Ciaran Carson was born in 1948 in Belfast. He has been awarded the *Irish Times* Literature Prize, the T.S. Eliot Prize and the *Yorkshire Post* Prize. *Shamrock Tea* was longlisted for the Booker Prize. Carson's prose books *Last Night's Fun, The Star Factory* and *Fishing for Amber* — form a body of work unique in Irish literature. He is currently working on a new translation of Dante's *Inferno*.

'Welcome to Carsonville. A literary labyrinth . . . Relax, let the writing's slip-stream lift and levitate you through a magical state of being, verbal alchemy and dream. Carson's world is unique. That we, the readers, remain receptive, compliant, plunging even more willingly through the vortex of Carson's narrative, is a measure of the marvel of his writing' *Scotsman*

'Composed of 101 short chapters, Carson's new book is an eccentric disquisition on the world ranging from colour pigmentation in paintings, to flying, the Arnolfini Marriage, Wittgenstein and Sherlock Holmes. *Shamrock Tea* is a marvellous, entirely idiosyncratic book' *Marie Claire*

'*Shamrock Tea* is a fluid mosaic: each chapter is named after a particular colour; many are devoted to the lives of individual saints; all are connected together by a series of serendipitous affinities and associations . . . page by page, it is a book that puts no rein or limit on its generous imaginings' *Times Literary Supplement*

'Ciaran Carson sets himself an ambitious task, but the imagination and story-juggling skills which characterised his previous novel, *Fishing for Amber,* have done him proud once again' *The Times*

'The writing is bright and pacey. The 101 chapters fly by, each one firmly written, none more than a few pages long. This is a novel devoted to play, serendipity, and inconsequentiality . . . a cerebral and sparkling performance' *Tablet*

'The pleasures of this utterly original work lie in the small narratives with which the larger narrative is spiced . . . an eccentric treat' *Daily Telegraph*

Also by Ciaran Carson

SHAMROCK
TEA

Ciaran Carson

Terry —
scratch your head
thru this one

[signature]

Granta Books
London · New York

Granta Publications, 2/3 Hanover Yard, London N1 8BE

First published in Great Britain by Granta Books 2001

This edition published by Granta Books 2002

A CIP catalogue record for this book is available from the
British Library.

1 3 5 7 9 10 8 6 4 2

Typeset in Perpetua by M Rules

Printed and bound in Great Britain by
Mackays of Chatham plc

He divided a panel into a hundred squares and marked them down, with numbered figures, in a small book, then painted these squares with various colours, various shades, greens, yellows, blues, flesh tints and other mixtures, giving the shaded tint of each one in so far as he could, and writing it down in the little book as aforesaid.

Karel van Mander, *Het Schilder-Boeck*, Haarlem, 1604

The world is everything that is the case.

Ludwig Wittgenstein, *Tractatus Logico-Philosophicus*, London, 1922

CONTENTS

1

PARIS GREEN

Perhaps I will return one day to the world I first entered. For now, I wish to record something of it, if only to remind myself of what I am.

The first things I remember are the colours of my bedroom wallpaper, and their chalky taste under my fingernails. It would, of course, be years before I learned what the shades were called, which leads me to my first paint-box. Hooker's Green, Vermilion, Prussian Blue, Burnt Sienna: I knew stories must lie behind those names, and I resolved to discover them some day.

As I learned to speak, I understood that green was the colour of jealousy. But I did not know yet that Napoleon, on the isle of St Helena, was supposed to have died from breathing the fumes of his bedroom wallpaper, which was liberally tinted with the arsenic-laced pigment known as Emerald, or Paris Green; nor did I know that a green moon shone in the sky for weeks after Krakatoa disintegrated on 28 August 1883, the feast day of St Monica, mother of St Augustine.

In the *Confessions*, Augustine speaks with awe of the vast cloisters of his memory, which is an immeasurable sanctuary for countless images of all kinds. Perplexed by time – since the present has no duration and past and future do not exist – he concludes that the measure of time must be memory; hence a long past is a long remembrance of the past.

In Church liturgy, which is a measure of time, green is the colour of hope, and the priest wears green vestments on the Sundays between Whitsuntide and Advent. When Nero, in his savage persecution of the Christians, had them sewn up in the skins of wild beasts, and exposed to the fury of dogs, he is reputed to have peered at the spectacle through a prism of green beryl, which has magnifying properties. Otherwise, green is the colour of the planet Venus, and therefore of love and fertility.

The Greeks thought green to be associated with Hermaphroditus, son of blue Hermes and yellow Aphrodite. Green is ambiguous. It is the colour of aliens, or of creatures who dwell in the underworld, as illustrated by the following legend:

On 20 July 1434, at the hour of tierce as told by the great Belfry of Bruges, in Flanders, two green-skinned twin children – a boy and a girl of about thirteen – materialized from a storm-grating in the town square, clothed in garments of what appeared to be frogskin. They were dripping wet. Crying bitterly, they were brought to the nearby house of Arnolfini, a respected Italian merchant. Questioning them in various languages and dialects, he found they responded well to Attic Greek. In their land, they said, it was always twilight. It was called St Martin's Land: that saint was much revered there, since he had descended from the upper world and made them Christians. Yesterday they had been tending their flocks of dragons and had followed them into a cave. They heard a sound of distant bells, in which they discerned the voices of angels calling to them. Led by the voices, they had climbed up a flight of steps roughly hewn in the rock, to emerge in a brilliant light.

The children were baptized. It was quickly established that they would eat no food save beans, and after several weeks of this diet their green hue noticeably diminished. Shortly afterwards, the boy died. The girl, who was somewhat wanton, lived long as a servant to the Arnolfini household. There is no further record of her fate; but it was noted, and remembered by the people of Bruges, that the day on which the green children had first come into this world was the feast of St Margaret of Antioch.

2

DRAGON'S BLOOD

Margaret, known as Marina to the Greeks, was a beautiful daughter of a heathen priest, Eddesius, of Antioch in Pisidia. When her father learned that she had embraced Christ, he disowned her, and she was forced to look after her nurse's flocks. One day, Olybrius, the Prefect of Pisidia, was out hunting when he spied Margaret with her sheep, and immediately desired her. He asked if she were free, or a slave: if free, he would marry her; if a slave, he would buy her.

She replied that she was a free-born woman, but a servant of Christ. Olybrius had her brought before a tribunal, on the charge of worshipping a false god. She was thrown into prison, where she was put to the rack and lacerated with rakes until her body spurted blood as from a fountain. Still she refused to submit to his lust. Alone in her cell, while her gaolers pondered further tortures for her, she was visited by the devil in the shape of a monstrous dragon, which opened its maw over her head, put out its tongue under her feet, and swallowed her in one gulp.

Fortunately, she was holding a cross, which grew to the size of a broadsword; and with this holy weapon she cut open the dragon's belly from within and emerged intact.

Another demon then appeared to her; but she wrestled with him, pinned him to the floor with her foot and commanded him to divulge his origin. He told her that he, and many others of his ilk, had been enclosed in a big brass chest by Solomon; but it had been found in Babylon and broken open by people looking for treasure, so that he and his fellow demons were released to plague the world.

The next day, Margaret was burned with torches, hung by the hair from a gibbet, and thrown into a vat of boiling oil. Five thousand of the spectators, impressed by her fortitude, were converted, and summarily executed by the authorities. Margaret herself was finally beheaded. Her executioner fell down dead immediately afterwards; not as a retribution, but as a reward whereby he would join her in heaven, for he had been most reluctant to perform his duty.

These events happened under the reign of the Emperor Diocletian, and were witnessed by one Theotimus, from whom we have the story. Theotimus and Margaret's nurse, writes Theotimus, were in the prison ministering to her bread and water. They looked in through a window, and in the fear of God noted everything that took place: Theotimus' account is therefore gospel truth.

'Margaret' means 'pearl', whose whiteness signifies virginity. The power of the pearl is said to work against effusions of the blood and against passions of the heart. Because she escaped unscathed from the belly of a monster, St Margaret is the patron of safe childbirth. It is considered most efficacious for pregnant women to touch her girdle, which is preserved intact in six locations in France alone. Likewise, at least eight well-authenticated heads of the saint exist throughout Christendom.

In art, her emblem is a dragon, sometimes of suitable dimensions to engorge a human being; but an anonymous fourteenth-century master of Bohemia has portrayed her with a little dragon perched on her wrist, like a falcon. Often, the dragon is knee-high to Margaret, like a pet dog; and it is thus that the saint and her escort are shown by Jan van Eyck, as a carved finial on the armchair beside the bed in the painting known as the Arnolfini Wedding, or the Arnolfini Double Portrait.

3

FLESH

My mother, solicitous for the welfare of my soul, as Monica had been for that of her son, St Augustine, gave me an illustrated *Lives of the Saints* for my eleventh birthday. I coloured in St Margaret's dragon with the Hooker's Green from my paint-box; I remember the name because I confused it with that of Richard Hooke who, I had just learned in school, had invented a superior form of telescope which he used to formulate the theory of planetary motion.

St Margaret's dress had to be vermilion. I am pleased now to note that vermilion derives from *vermiculus*, the Latin for 'little worm'; for this red dye was once prepared from the crushed bodies of female scale insects of the genus *Kermes*. Vermilion was also known as St John's Blood, because in Germany the kermes were traditionally collected by serfs, fortified by copious draughts of St John's Wort, between eleven and twelve midnight on the eve of 29 August, the feast of St John's beheading.

The *Lives of the Saints* resided, together with the other items in my small library, in a bookcase made from an orange-box placed on its end: thus my books, when opened, emanated a lingering scent of oranges, which I confused with that of church incense, for oranges were often cited in the sermons given by the Redemptorist Fathers in their missions to the Catholic laity of Belfast.

The typical Redemptorist scenario would find a thirsty boy in the summer holidays alone outside a greengrocer's shop. Here he would gaze at a beautiful display of oranges. He would contemplate their dimpled peel as, warmed by the sun, their aroma wafted over him, summoning a mental image of his biting into one, registering the tiny spits of zest on the roof of his mouth. Then, considering his thirst, he would go further, and begin to think of divesting the fruit to expose its dripping segments, as the boundary between thought and deed began to waver.

Now the orange, palpably within hand's reach, weighed on his mind. And no one, he could see, was watching him. The greengrocer was engrossed by two customers, who wanted to know the relative merits of the new British and the Dublin Queens. The policeman had just entered the public house next door. A motor car droned by through the empty sunstruck street. No one, thought the boy, was watching him. So he put out his hand and slipped the orange into the pocket of his trousers. After all, no one had been watching him; and it was only one orange among many. But God, concluded the Redemptorist – here he would draw a crucifix from his black belt and hold it aloft in a panoptic flourish – God was watching that boy, and to God, who sees all, nothing is without significance; to Him, the One is Many.

Oranges were thus associated in my mind with theft, or loss. So I thought it politic, when I acquired my orange-box book-case, to make a pre-emptive prayer to St Antony of Padua, who is invoked as the finder of lost or stolen articles. He achieved this reputation when one of his disciples, after borrowing a book belonging to Antony without his permission, was visited by a terrible apparition which commanded him on pain of death to return it.

St Antony's reputation for preaching was unparalleled; and such was the speed of his progress from place to place, that many intelligent witnesses were convinced of his ubiquity. Thirty-two years after his death in 1231, his remains were translated to Padua. The flesh was all consumed except the tongue, which was found incorrupt, red, and as fresh as it was while he was still living.

4

SCARLET

When a saint died, there was considerable tumult among the populace. At Padua, throughout the months of June and July 1231, night and day, long processions spontaneously formed near the convent of Arcela, where the body of St Antony lay in an open catafalque, surrounded by white lilies.

Church bells tolled incessantly, confusing night and day. Many of the faithful heard angelic voices. Strange clouds wheeled above the towers of the city, perplexing the most gifted of nephelo-mancers. Lofty trees of wax swayed on platforms borne by chanting men, and on floats drawn by oxen through the portals of the city. Candles burned ubiquitously. In this zone where normal time had been suspended, a collective delirium reigned, as every-one – princes and beggars alike – sought a memento of the saint.

To acquire a corporeal relic was problematic even for those present at the decease; but transcendental contact with the saint – even long after death – could be achieved by touching a cloth to his clothes, or the ground on which he had stood, the straw on which he had slept, his tomb, his relic, his images. Oil or wax from the lights of the shrines were used to anoint the affected parts of one's body. Water was drunk that had washed the saint's corpse. At the shrine of St Antony, wine was passed over the relics, diluted, and administered to patients in homoeopathic doses.

So the influence of a saint could be maintained over many centuries. My mother possessed one such relic, of St Thérèse, the Little Flower of Lisieux: a tiny swatch of faintly stained beige linen which had touched the body of Thérèse, or touched a cloth touched to her clothes, glued to a faded red plush background within a glass-faced brass receptacle about the diameter of a lip-salve tin, or a small watch. Applied to anyone suffering from a bad chest cold, the relic invariably proved efficacious, since Thérèse had died of tuberculosis and was therefore the patron of bronchial complaints.

The reliquary was kept in a little drawer in the writing cabinet in the front room, together with other mementoes: a green-lipped mussel shell inscribed on its inner surface with the words 'Portrush 1944' in violet indelible ink (a souvenir of my parents' honeymoon); a milk tooth (mine); a set of Wills' Woodbine cigarette cards depicting the medicinal plants of the British Isles; and a bottle of Rescue Remedy with an eye-dropper stopper. There were other drawers besides this one, and pigeon-holes and compartments, each containing different narrative implications. Tucked into a sheaf of ancient postcards was a postcard-size photograph of my mother and father, hand-tinted so that they both appeared rouged and lipsticked, their eyes an identical doll blue.

This last item had been produced by my uncle Celestine, an amateur camera buff, a philatelist, and an avid reader of detective and gothic fiction, as epitomized by the works of Arthur Conan Doyle and Edgar Allan Poe. For my twelfth birthday he gave me an omnibus edition of the Sherlock Holmes stories. To a great mind, says Holmes in *A Study in Scarlet*, nothing is little; and from a drop of water, he maintained, a logician could infer the possibility of an Atlantic or a Niagara, without having seen or heard of one or the other; for all life is a great chain, the nature of which is known when we are shown a single link of it.

5

GALLAHER'S BLUE

Our family name of Carson is perceived as an unusual one for Catholics; for it is invariably associated with Protestant Unionism, as exemplified by Lord Duncairn, Edward Carson, who is thought by many to be the founder of the state of Northern Ireland. I was told, when I had attained the use of reason, that my paternal great-grandfather had been a Presbyterian who converted and imbued his offspring with such zeal that my grandfather proceeded to name his sons after popes of Rome.

Hence Celestine, after Celestine V, patron saint of book-binders; my father, Sylvester, after the brilliant scholar Sylvester II, pioneer of the abacus and the pneumatic organ; and the black sheep of the family, Leo, who had run off to America before I was born, was named after Leo II, who, on St Mark's Day, 25 April 799, miraculously survived an attempt by a rival papal faction to cut out his eyes and tongue.

Yet Celestine, in particular, maintained an ambivalence

towards the memory of the famous Carson. He had an ancient press clipping from the Belfast *Newsletter* of 10 October 1923, featuring a photograph of Lord Duncairn cutting the first sod at a ceremony to mark the foundation of the embankment of the new Silent Valley dam in the Mourne Mountains. My uncle maintained that the cigarette the elegantly garbed Lord was holding between the first and second fingers of his right hand was a Gallaher's 'Blue': a recent biographer had proved it, by making a microscopic study of the apparent texture of its ash.

Furthermore, the plant attached to the sod could be identified as *Tussilago farfara*, the Coltsfoot, from the characteristic hoof shape of its leaves. It is known also as Poor Man's Tobacco, Dummy-weed, Coughwort, and Wild Rhubarb; its leaves are the basis of the British Herb Tobacco, the other ingredients being Buckbean, Eyebright, Betony, Rosemary, Thyme, Lavender, and Camomile flowers. When he was not smoking 'Blues', Celestine would resort to a similar herbal mix, which he jokingly referred to as 'Shamrock Tea'.

During Lent his home would be suffused with its aroma, almost masking the forensic whiff that emanated from his darkroom, and the sacramental odour of the fixatives he prepared for his tinted photographs, ground from essences of lavender and terebinthine, gum elemi, and virgin wax. He scorned those who simply used the watercolours from a child's wafer-box. The principles of Cennino Cennini, the last spokesman of the medieval tradition, he argued, were still relevant today: to paint faces, the flesh must first be underpainted with the pale green earth, *terre verte*, and the pink flesh tones hatched thinly on top, working in progressively paler shades from shadow to light; the green was allowed to show through in the half-tones, and nicely imitated the pearly tones of real flesh.

In a brief flirtation with tempura, he had proved Cennino's assertion that the pale yolk of a town hen's egg was most suitable for painting the faces of young people with cool fresh colours, while the darker yolk of a country hen's egg was to be preferred for aged or swarthy persons. To illustrate his point he showed me a retouched print of his only child, my cousin Berenice, whom I had barely noticed until then. She was portrayed as Cleopatra, in a costume apparently contrived from some old silk scarves and a feather boa. Her teeth appeared to have a greenish tinge, and I determined to look more closely at her when next I saw her.

I am almost sure that the photograph I have still of her and me, dated 24 July 1959 on the back, marks that occasion. It was also the feast of Christina the Astonishing, patron saint of psychiatrists.

6

LAVENDER

Born to a family of high degree, orphaned at the age of fifteen, Christina became increasingly prone to cataleptic fits, until one day she was pronounced dead by her uncle's physician. Her body was laid out in sumptuous style, covered with white lilies and encased in a brass sarcophagus. At the *Agnus Dei* of her requiem the lid of the coffin flew open and the body of Christina was seen to levitate slowly to the rafters. The mourners fled in horror, save for one brave priest who, crucifix in hand, conjured her to come down.

She told him that she had been so offended by the odour of the congregation that she had found it necessary to fly away from it. She had lately visited Hell, where the stench of corruption was so thick that it served to fuel the infernal light. She had visited Purgatory, too, where the smell was not as bad, and had seen friends in both places. Then she went to Heaven, which smelled of rosemary smoke and lavender. It was there that she heard the priest at her funeral mass intone the *Agnus Dei*, whereupon she thought herself back to earth.

On her return to the world, Christina found human society difficult to bear. She was tormented throughout her life by her acute olfactory sense. Even the company of one body was problematic, for it would be contaminated by the scent of others it had been with. Hence she was wont to take herself off to high places, and was seen to perch on weathervanes, or in the tops of trees. Eventually, her guardians built a tower for her, where she remained until she died a second time; though other accounts maintain she was shot down with arrows on one of her afternoon flights.

In my copy of the *Lives of the Saints*, Christina is depicted holding a tower like Rapunzel's in one hand, and an arrow in the other. I can easily find the page, for it is marked by the photograph of Berenice and me. It is summer. We are standing knee-high in the long grass of the derelict allotments at the north end of the old Belfast Waterworks, a few hundred yards from Celestine's house. Though the photograph is not coloured, I know I am wearing a jacket of light green tweed with flecks of lavender and oatmeal in it, an open-necked white shirt, a green and red striped elastic belt with a snake clasp, and grey flannels. She has on a faded pink sleeveless frock printed with apple-blossom. We are smiling.

Years later, I was to come across these remarks by the philosopher, Ludwig Wittgenstein:

I saw in a photograph (not a colour photograph) a boy with slicked-back blond hair and a dirty light-coloured jacket, and a man with dark hair standing in front of a machine – a kind of lathe – which was made in part of castings painted black, and in part of finished, smooth axles, gears, etc., and next to it a grating made of light galvanized wire. I saw the twisted iron surfaces as iron-coloured, the boy's hair as blond, the castings as black, the grating zinc-coloured, despite the fact that everything is depicted simply in lighter and darker tones of the photographic paper.

Wittgenstein's favourite recreation was going to the 'flicks', as he liked to call them. He particularly enjoyed westerns and musicals. His favourite film stars were Carmen Miranda and Betty Hutton. He disliked British films intensely, claiming that their depiction of reality was unconvincing. Hollywood, on the other hand, was 'the real thing'.

7

PEARL

Celestine's portrait of my cousin turned out to be inaccurate: Berenice's teeth were a brilliant pearl-drop white, emphasized, it seemed to me, by the slight lisp of her voice. As I got to know her, I began to think myself fond of her. She was like a boy in many respects, and her stamp collection contained many beautiful items: I think especially of her complete set, together with some typographical variations, of the first Irish Provisional issues, which consisted of overprinted British stamps, and the rare Holy Year error of 18 September 1933, in which the Adoration of the Cross is printed upside-down.

Underneath it, Berenice had written, in a careful italic round-hand: *The Feast of St Joseph of Cupertino, Patron Saint of Flying. d. 18 September 1663. A.M.D.G.* This saint, indeed, was a popular icon of the times: flying was just beginning to come within the reach of the ordinary man and woman, or at least those in the middle classes; and most of the faithful were quite familiar with the legend of the 'flying friar'. Joseph's father was a carpenter, called

Joseph himself, but he was so poor that Joseph Minor was born in a manger in a lean-to shed, for the house itself had been claimed by the Crown bailiffs.

The boy Joseph was famously absent-minded and inert. He was usually to be seen standing on street corners with his mouth hanging open, earning him the nickname 'Boccaperta', or 'Open Gub'. The only job he could do was to sweep the street in front of the local taverna, whose clientele would humour him with the odd tip. Nevertheless, his life was to become one long succession of ecstasies and supernatural happenings on a scale unparalleled in the reasonably authenticated life of any other saint.

Though apparently dim-witted, Joseph was notably devout. He was often to be seen in the company of priests, who tolerated him as a simple soul. After some years, out of pity, they allowed him to sit an examination for the priesthood. Miraculously, he was presented with the only text he was fit to read. Thereafter he progressed by leaps and bounds. During his seventeen years as a Franciscan monk at the abbey of Grotella, over seventy of his levitations were witnessed and recorded by men of unimpeachable integrity. On one occasion, the friars were building a calvary. The middle cross of the three was thirty-six feet high, and correspondingly heavy, defying the efforts of ten men to lift it. St Joseph is said to have flown, with incredible rapidity, seventy yards to the cross, whereupon he picked it up as if it were a straw and lowered it into place.

Eventually, his life became surrounded by such disturbing phenomena that the Church authorities felt compelled to restrain him. The Neapolitan inquisitors accused him of 'drawing a rabble after him like a new Messiah'. In addition to his levitations he was wont to suffer ecstasies from which blows, burning with candles, and pinpricks failed to arouse him. Incurably hypersensitive to religion, for thirty-five years he was not allowed to celebrate Mass in public, to keep choir, to take his meals with his brethren, or to attend any public function. In effect, he was imprisoned in a series of increasingly remote and secluded locations. Deserted by man, but visited daily by God, Joseph of Cupertino fell sick on 10 August 1663, the feast of St Lawrence, who was martyred on a gridiron. Joseph rallied briefly to make his final levitation on 15 August, the feast of the Assumption of Our Blessed Lady into Heaven. He died on 18 September, the object of both official reserve and popular veneration.

8

TOBACCO

How can I describe Berenice, as she was then? The photograph is only one appearance. I remember her, for instance, in a Black Watch tartan knee-length skirt that matches her dark Cleopatra-cut hair and her grass-green eyes. Over a cream broderie anglaise blouse she is wearing a bottle-green wool cardigan, shop-bought because her mother, who would otherwise have likely knitted it, had died some years before.

Her fingernails are bitten. The thumb and forefinger of her left hand are stained with violet ink, and she has drawn a violet watch on the other wrist. It is ten to two. There is a scab on her right knee, a relic of her falling as she skidded on her way to early morning Mass a week ago, for she was wearing the new one-strap, low-heeled, patent leather shoes she has on now, and the soles had not yet lost their slipperiness; now, the toes are already a bit scuffed. Her ears are pierced: I can see the tiny cushioned pinholes in the lobes; she has no earrings in today.

I remember these details because, the night before, I had read the Sherlock Holmes story 'The Cardboard Box'. If you are familiar with the plot you will know that the box (a yellow honeydew tobacco box) contained two severed ears, one of which – a man's – was pierced. Moreover, the box had been posted in Belfast, the city in which I lived, making the circumstances of the story all the more authentic. So I could not help but focus on Berenice's ears that day; and visualizing them now, I am drawn to see the rest of her.

As Holmes states elsewhere: the ideal reasoner would, when he had once been shown a single fact in all its bearings, deduce from it not only the chain of events which led up to it but also all the results which would follow from it. As Cuvier could correctly describe a whole animal from the contemplation of one bone, so the observer who has thoroughly understood one link in a series of incidents should be able to accurately state all the other ones, both before and after.

I follow Berenice in my mind's eye; or I think myself to be in my former body, standing beside her. We are in the Waterworks, leaning against a tumbledown shed in the derelict allotments. From the pocket of her green cardigan she produces a mock tortoiseshell cigarette-case, snapping it open with a conspiratorial one-handed flourish. Inside are two Gallaher's 'Blues', which she puts between her lips and lights with one match, like the leading man of a Hollywood film. I am impressed by her sophistication.

She would make, I think, an excellent heroine in a girl's adventure story, like those in the *School Friend*, a weekly magazine I had scorned out of male prejudice, till I realized I was increasingly fascinated by its costume dramas, featuring, for instance, the beautiful princess of Transylvania, who was wont to don peasant garb the better to mingle with and know her subjects; or the Silent Three of the Lower Fourth, who cowled themselves in monks' habits nightly to flit through secret passages under the ancient school in search of the truth behind a current mystery.

Berenice seems to me to be smiling inwardly. When she tells me that she has found a way to levitate, I am not altogether surprised; there appear to be no limits to her resourcefulness. She will reveal the secret on her birthday, 18 August, which happens to be the feast of St Helena, mother of the Emperor Constantine, and finder of the True Cross.

9

Rust

We are assured by the unanimous tradition of English historians that Helena was born in Colchester, for she was the daughter of King Cole, who gave his name to that city. In the year 326 she was granted a vision by the Holy Ghost in which she saw the Cross buried within Calvary, and she set off for Jerusalem forthwith. Here she found that the heathens had built their temples on Calvary, the better to conceal the place where Christ had been entombed. She tore down the temples and broke the statues of Jupiter and Venus. Upon digging to a great depth, her entourage discovered the holy sepulchre, and near it three crosses.

A little way off they found the three holy nails, which were somewhat rusted, and the title which had been fixed to the Cross; so it was impossible to tell which of the three crosses was the one on which Our Saviour had given up his life. The bishop Macarius, being made aware of the dilemma, suggested to Helena that she bring the three crosses to one of the principal ladies in the city, who lay mortally ill. This was done, and Macarius applied the crosses singly to the patient, who immediately and perfectly recovered after the touch of one of the crosses, the other two having been tried without effect.

St Helena enclosed the main part of the Cross in a silver shrine in the Church of the Holy Sepulchre. It has been asserted repeatedly that there are enough relics of the Cross to build a man-of-war. It is sufficient to say, to refute this ignorant calumny, that the particles of the Holy Cross are often as minute as the head of a pin, or as fine as a hair. Or we may choose to believe the testimony of Paulinus, in his epistle to Severus, that though chips were almost daily cut off from the Cross, it thereby suffered no diminution. St Cyril of Jerusalem, writing twenty-five years later, noted that bits of the relic were scattered throughout Christendom; and he likens this wonder to the miraculous feeding of the five thousand, as attested by Scripture.

Of the nails, St Helena set one in a bridle and another in a diadem for her son. The third she threw into the Adriatic Gulf in order to calm a storm, which sea is under her protection to this day. When she died, the Emperor Constantine ordered her to be buried with much pomp in a stately mausoleum. He erected a statue to her memory; and she is further commemorated by the island of St Helena, discovered by Spanish sailors on her feast day, where another emperor, Napoleon, would later die in exile.

Appropriately, her feast day is also that of Clare of Montefalco, the Augustinian nun who relived and sought to reproduce within her body the principal stages in the agony of Christ, from Gethsemane to Golgotha. It was widely believed that Christ had planted his Cross in her heart. So, following her death, she had hardly breathed her last when the sisters of the convent flung themselves on her still-warm body to retrieve the precious heart. When they had cut her open with a kitchen knife, they found in her body the insignia of the Passion: first the Cross, then the scourge, the lance, the sponge, the pillar of flagellation, the crown of thorns, and the purple robe.

Image begets image. Helena saw the Cross suspended in inner, earthly space; Clare conceived the Cross within her inner space; and reality corroborated these visions. I still dream of Berenice. We float through the cloisters of memory, looking for our waking selves.

10

SERPENTINE

It is 18 August 1959: Uncle Celestine is preparing the magic lantern show he has devised for Berenice's birthday party: a brief history of the Silent Valley dam, the main water supply for the city of Belfast. It is a subject which has long fascinated him, for he sees in it a paradigm of our civil disturbances. He is smoking a Gallaher's 'Blue'.

Dusk begins to fall. He pulls the curtains and lights the lantern. The first slide looks north from the main embankment.

As to why the Silent Valley should be so called, says Celestine, there is a legend that no birds ever sang there. It is believed by some that this phenomenon is connected to the presence of peculiar air pockets which interfere with flight. High emissions of radioactivity have been detected in the area, and certain rocks are said to glow at night.

The blue smoke from Celestine's cigarette unfurls upwards through the funnel of light as he moves to the second image.

Here is Lord Carson being presented with a fine specimen of

hexagonal quartz, which is thought to represent the six counties of the newly created state of Northern Ireland; rocks of the neighbourhood, says Celestine, known as the Diamond Rocks, are veined with many beautiful crystals of amethyst, topaz, chrysoberyl, tourmaline and peridot.

He shows a close-up of examples of the said crystals, which I recognize from the collection in the Ulster Museum. They shimmer in the dark of the parlour.

The olive-green peridot, he says, is especially prized when it occurs as serpentine, from which figurines of St Patrick banishing the snakes from Ireland are carved.

Next, a fine view of Slieve Donard, the highest peak in the Mourne region. Note the ruins of the stone hermitage, just visible on the summit; for this is where St Donard made his abode, after his conversion by St Patrick. It is related that Donard was the pagan chief of the district. St Patrick, being newly arrived there, sent an acolyte to Donard, asking for provisions for his retinue; for holy men expected that such dues should be paid to them. Donard told the boy to take one of his fiercest bulls. The boy attempted to take the bull, and was duly chased.

Here we have a magnificent specimen of an Irish bull. You will remember from your Irish history that the bull is an emblem of Ulster, being the object of the famous Cattle Raid of Cooley. When St Patrick's boy told him what had happened, the saint gave him a magic halter, which enabled him to lead the animal away like a lamb to the slaughter. It was killed, cut into joints, and salted.

A diagram of the various cuts of beef, which I have reproduced from the *Household Oracle*, published by Hutchinson &

Co., of London. Sirloin. Rump. Shoulder. Brisket. Clod. I should point out that these are English cuts, and might not correspond precisely to those familiar to the butchers of ancient Ireland; but the general picture is clear.

The next day Donard complained to Patrick that he had stolen his bull. If your Lordship says so, said St Patrick, you shall have your bull back again. He made the sign of the cross, and the various cuts of meat that had been the bull were immediately reconstituted. He breathed into the bull's mouth, and it was restored to life. Shortly afterwards, Donard asked to be baptized, but not before confessing his difficulty with the doctrine of the Trinity. Patrick plucked a shamrock from the ground, and held it up as illustration: a plant with one stem, but three leaves of equal status. It would become the emblem of Ireland.

11

BLOOD GREEN

Berenice nudged my knee with hers. She knew from past experience that her father was only warming to his theme, and that the
illustrated lecture had some considerable time to go. I could see,
too, that he was oblivious to his audience. Two of the party guests
had fallen asleep; the other three were happily absorbed in chew-
ing their way through a bowl of Callard & Bowser's Rum and
Butter toffees. It was time to leave.

Berenice slipped out the door. Some minutes later I followed
her into the dark hallway. She put her finger to her lips and took
my hand. We tiptoed up the stairs. We came to the threshold of
Celestine's study; I hesitated, but she pulled me in and turned the
key in the lock. She pointed to a picture on the wall above
Celestine's desk. It showed a couple in medieval clothing standing in a room: the man in a dark outfit, holding the hand of the
woman in green. The man's eyes were heavily lidded, seeming to
look sidelong away from the viewer. Hers were modestly downcast. His nostrils were flared.

Berenice stretched up and pressed one of the beads in the moulding of the picture frame. It gave way with a snub click, and the whole picture swung open to reveal a cubby-hole built into the wall. Inside was a clay pipe with a thimble-sized bowl, and an emerald enamel snuff-box inlaid with a harp and shamrock motif. She took it out and opened it. The inside of the lid was engraved

A.O.H.

Shamrock Tea

A.M.D.G.

Instead of the familiar whiff of Celestine's herbal tobacco, this stuff breathed a different incense: dark, pungent, bitter, deep, composed of many different strands of faded greens and sepias. She took down the pipe and clicked the picture back into place.

It won't work unless you look at the picture, she said. She tamped some of the stuff into the clay thimble, lit it with a match from Celestine's desk, and drew on it till it began to glow. She took a few puffs and handed it to me. I inhaled deeply and felt the smoke catch the back of my throat.

She swivelled her eyes towards the picture; I followed her gaze. For a split second I had double vision; I blinked; the picture glimmered in its frame, then resolved itself into a stereoscopic depth. The folds and pleats of the lady's green gown stood out vividly against the scarlet background of the bed. I could almost feel the fur fringes of the man's dark crimson-purple robe, the palpable brim and rounded crown of his hat. Then I noticed the convex mirror hanging on the wall behind the couple, showing their backs, behind which, telescopically reflected, were two further figures, one dressed in blue, the other in red, poised on the threshold of the room, about to enter its dimension.

Berenice took my hand. I became aware of her pulse, and my own seeming to reciprocate hers. I felt the smoke course through my veins, and thought of my blood being turned green, green entering the red as if swirled in the glass barrel of a hypodermic. Berenice began to hum – no tune I could recognize, maintaining a flat arabesque of melody – and as she hummed, I felt my soles vibrate with a wobbly underfoot pressure. It took me a second or two to realize that we were an inch or two adrift of the floorboards.

We floated slowly upwards. When our heads were level with those in the picture, we became the figures in the picture.

12

BLUE ROCKET

I can now regard these events with the hindsight of a little knowledge. The literature of psychotropia is vast, and I have hardly penetrated its nearer reaches; but I have some experience in the field, corroborated by the few examples I note below.

The hagiographers of St Joseph of Cupertino have written that for a period of five years he tasted neither bread nor wine; and on Fridays the green herbs he ate were so distasteful that only he could use them. It is further recorded that many of the saint's levitations occurred on Fridays; and one unorthodox authority maintains that Joseph was familiar with the ingredients of witches' flying potions, taken as a salve or hypodermically. Invariably, these are described as being green in colour.

One formula involves Parsley, Poplar leaves and soot; another, Water Parsnip, Deadly Nightshade, Cinquefoil, and bat's blood. The Thorn-apple, *Datura stramonium*, also known as Angels' Trumpets, or Devils' Trumpets, features largely in some recipes.

Culpeper recommends Thorn-apple to be taken for epilepsy and convulsions.

Other ingredients include Henbane, Aconite and Sweet Flag. Henbane – Devil's Eye, or Stinking Roger – is the source of hyoscyamine, which Dr Crippen used to poison Mrs Crippen. It was known to Dioscorides as Pythonion; Pliny considered it a dangerous medicine. When, according to Ovid, the Scythian women sprinkled their bodies with it, they grew feathers. Elsewhere he tells of how the dead in Hades wear crowns of Henbane, as they hopelessly explore the dreary environs of the Styx.

Aconite – Monkshood, Wolfsbane, or Blue Rocket – is also known as Birds of Paradise. It slows the heartbeat, and some have thought, by taking it, to live eternally. Werewolves can be killed with arrows dipped in Aconite. Ovid says that when Cerberus, the three-headed dog, was dragged by Hercules to be chained to the portal of the Underworld, it howled three times, and foamed at the mouth; and where the foam fell on the black soil, it grew yellow flowers. These were the Aconites from which Medea brewed a poison for Theseus.

Sweet Flag – *Acorus calamus* – is called Green Flag in Ireland, where it is thought to confer second sight. It is one of the ingredients of the Holy Ointment delivered to Moses by God; Dioscorides records its being smoked, like Coltsfoot, to clear the bronchial passageways, or to induce visions. Sweet Flag is also Holy Rush, St Michael's Sword, and Angel's Wing. It is a member of the *Arum* family, and hence a cousin of Green Dragon; another relative, *Calamus draco*, the East Indian palm discovered by the Jesuits, yields the red lac known to colourmen as Dragon's Blood.

Not many years ago, Professor Erich Wolfgang Köhl, then Professor of Metaphysics at the University of Louvain in Belgium, prepared a flying potion based on his researches into Flemish folklore. He and some colleagues rubbed this ointment into their groins and armpits. Before long, they found themselves flying through the air at great speed over a darkened landscape in which strange rituals were being enacted. Afterwards, some informants spoke of clouds boiling and swirling, of leaves, quite unlike ordinary leaves, billowing and falling through the universe.

Common to all these accounts is the suspicion that these herbs confer invisibility, as well as the ability to fly.

13

ORANGE

There was a scent of oranges in the painted room. I felt the dangling weight of the rich garments which clothed me, the cool damp lining of the ponderous hat. As for the lady who was Berenice, her dark hair was now golden, wound into horns surrounded by small plaits, the horns caught in finely woven red nets, all covered in a veil of fluted white linen. Her long green gown was trimmed with fur, the blue damask sleeves of her underdress gathered at the wrists into bands of gold and pink braid.

I turned towards the source of the orange aroma. One fruit lay on its reflection in the window-sill; another three were congregated on the lid of a coffer. Beyond the window was a tree with cherries growing on it, a glimpse of blue sky. By the angle of the shadow on the embrasure, it must have been about noon on a summer's day. Even so, a single candle burned in the fretted brass chandelier.

Curiouser and curiouser, said Berenice.

It was also strange that we could not see back into Uncle Celestine's study; nor could we see the two figures which should have confronted us, according to the mirror we saw on the back wall of the painting, when we were looking at the painting. In fact, we could see nothing at all but a grey, formless blur.

I made to touch it with my hand and felt a palpable electric shock. The grey veil shimmered and buzzed, and drew itself back to show an open door to a steep staircase going down. Gingerly, supporting each other, unaccustomed to the language of our new bodies, we teetered across the pine floor, I in the long-toed wooden clogs I'd just put on, she in the red leather pattens under the more-than-body-length gown. We clambered awkwardly down to find ourselves in an Irish farmyard.

The smell was unmistakable. Turf smoke, pigs and cabbages. A broken tractor leaned against a wall beside a rusted harrow. A man was poised above a bale of hay with a pitchfork, making ready to stab it, but immobilized in the act. An arabesque of blue smoke trailed from the farmhouse chimney like writing. A paralysed cock balanced on one leg on the midden with his head thrown back.

Above us loomed a blue mountain range whose profile I knew from afar. We were in the Mournes, in a time which looked much like our own, not light years away from Uncle Celestine's study. All that remained to us was to find our way back. We could still levitate. We grasped hands, lifted ourselves, and found we could fly. In no time we were hundreds of feet up.

From this perspective, things looked like a map, plotted in little bits and pieces, ploughland and fallow, grass, gorse and plantations, elaborately joined up and kept apart by mazes of Ulster stone walls. Whitewashed farmsteads with high walls and barred gates around them were dotted strategically across the landscape, as were church steeples flying Union Jacks. Herds of strawberry cows grazed the lush grasses of the lower drumlin country. Flocks of thin sheep inhabited the higher pastures.

Just as I was thinking how beautifully ordered everything was, a thermal swept us off our intended course. Struggle as we might, we could not avoid being veered in towards the mountains. Inexorably, as if magnetized, we were drawn into the Silent Valley. We recognized it easily from Celestine's slide: a classic glacial U-shape, its steep walls lined with waterfalls and tumbling rills, all flowing into the miles-long artificial lake.

As we hovered above it, the pewter-coloured surface began to shimmer, as if coming to a boil. We began to lose power. Before we knew it, we were falling. We smashed through the pane of water. I had a glimpse of Berenice's elaborate green dress billowing over her head. Then everything went black.

14

RAVEN

According to my uncle Celestine, ever since the Mourne catchment area had been acquired by the Belfast Water Commissioners
in 1893, persistent rumours had circulated that a reservoir would
never be built in the Silent Valley. Secret tests had proved that the
valley had no rock bottom. It was the track of an ancient glacier,
and was so full of swallow-holes that it could never be made a
watertight dam. The case of St Donard's Well, on the nearby
summit of Slieve Donard, seemed to corroborate these stories,
for it is purported to have an internal connection, through the
core of the mountain, with the sea-shore south of Newcastle,
emerging at St Donard's Cave.

Once upon a time two fishermen had gone deep into this
cave, but they were met by the saint, who admonished them of
their folly. They recognized him immediately, for he was the
image of his statue in St Donard's church. He told them they had
trespassed the border between this world and the next, for the
cave was his peculiar residence until the Day of Judgement,

when he would appear with St Patrick to lead the Irish into Paradise.

On another occasion, a shepherd let fall his crook into Donard's Well; it was found two weeks later floating in Lough Neagh, some forty miles north. Similar phenomena were associated with other holy wells or lakes on other mountain tops, such as Slemish in Co. Antrim, and Slieve Gullion in Co. Armagh; and many diligent researchers were convinced that the whole of Northern Ireland was riddled with interconnecting subterranean channels.

Moreover, claimed Celestine, it was not without significance that the original order for the acquisition of the Silent Valley catchment area had been signed on 11 July 1893, the eve of the commemoration of William of Orange's victory at the Battle of the Boyne, and the feast of St Benedict, patron of speleologists and engineers.

Benedict was born in 480, in the ancient Sabine town of Nursia. Of his twin sister, the dedicated maiden Scholastica, we know little; but it is certain that they were buried in the same grave, for their minds and souls had forever been united. Towards the close of the century Benedict was sent to Rome for his studies, but the disturbed and profligate life of the city drove him to seek solitude. He climbed into the mountains, till he arrived at a place known as Subiaco, i.e., Sublacum, from the artificial lake built by Claudius, who dammed the waters of the Anio. There he met a monk called Romanus, who advised him how to become a hermit, providing him with a sheepskin garment, and leading him to an almost inaccessible cave.

Although he was occasionally mistaken for a wild animal by passing shepherds, Benedict's reputation for sanctity and wisdom eventually became such that he was importuned to descend from his desolate cavern. He established a community of monks at Subiaco; about the year 530, he withdrew from thence to Monte Cassino, near Naples, where he founded the greatest monastery the world has ever known.

As recorded by his hagiographer, St Gregory, the life of Benedict abounds in miracles. Standing one night, praying by his window, he experienced a vision whereby the whole world seemed to be gathered in one sunbeam, and brought thus before his eyes; for to him who is granted the light of eternity, all things are that light; and therefore every point in the universe can be visited from every other point.

St Benedict's emblem is a raven.

15

IRISH ROSE

Berenice and I were found in the early hours of 19 August, the feast of St Sebald of Nürnberg, who is invoked against death by exposure. We were lying unconscious, covered in green slime, on the embankment of the Belfast Waterworks Lower Reservoir, about a hundred yards from my uncle Celestine's house.

In the inquest that followed our return to consciousness, we claimed that, feeling sick after eating some of the party food, we had gone to the Waterworks for some fresh air and, overcome by nausea, had fallen in. We did not think of this as a lie; we were still understandably confused about our whereabouts, and one story seemed as good as another. Celestine, indeed, collaborated willingly enough with this fiction, though we suspected that he knew the truth.

We were confined to our separate beds. I cannot speak for Berenice at this point, but for some weeks I lay in a fever, unable to discriminate between dimensions. As I lay on my back, the bedroom ceiling became an especially interesting zone, whose magnified pits and dimples could be examined like a map. Mentally, I would invert and shrink myself to walk across its territory, spending hours exploring its crevasses, or ages crossing a lunar sea.

From time to time the room would be bathed in an amber glow, as if seen through the cellophane wrap of a Lucozade bottle. Shadows from the world beyond the window flickered over the rose-on-trellis wallpaper, as it became a serial adventure. Each petal had its bit part to play in the elaborate plot. Great campaigns were fought, in which the Irish, camouflaged as creeping flowers and leaves, were not always on the losing side.

I am reminded, now, of Leonardo's advice to painters: You should fix your eyes, he says, on certain walls stained with damp. You will see in these the likenesses of divine landscapes, adorned with mountains, ruins, rocks, extensive plains; and you will see there battles and strange figures engaged in violent actions. For in such walls the same thing happens as in the sound of church bells, in whose reverberations you may find every word imaginable.

Sometimes, come dusk, the corners of the room would be inhabited by unseen presences; subliminal things lurked under the bed. In the twilit borderland that is not yet sleep, I would feel my body oppressed by a faceless weight, my skin constellated by immeasurably dense pin-points. I heard voices.

I began to sleepwalk. In my dreams I wandered the colonnaded spaces of a vast cathedral echoing with dim organ music, or was lost in a city that did not quite resemble my own. Some quarters seemed familiar, till I realized they belonged to cities I had read about in books. The spires, the minarets, the golden

44

tabernacles: all were false. I ran from them, pursued by dog-headed gods.

I'd wake to feel the cold of the kitchen tiles on my bare feet, or I'd come to, struggling in the wardrobe, looking for a portal in its back. On one such night, I woke on the bedroom floor. The bed-clothes and mattress had been dragged off the bed. There, on the wire base, I saw the picture of a female saint. In one hand she held a sword; in the other, a chain fastened to the neck of a little demon crouching at her feet. My mother, it transpired, had hidden this image beneath the mattress for my protection: for this was St Dympna, patron of sleepwalkers, and of the insane.

16

SNOW WHITE

Dympna was the Christian daughter of a pagan king of Oriel, in Ireland. Her beautiful mother fell mortally ill. As she lay dying, she made the king swear he would never remarry, unless it was to someone who looked exactly like herself. After the funeral the king sent messengers to scour the country for such a person. None was found, but on their return the messengers noticed that Dympna was the living image of the dead queen. Her hair was raven-black, her skin as white as snow, as her mother's had been. The king took it into his head that he must marry his daughter. She repelled all his advances.

Day and night he importuned her. In desperation, Dympna turned to her venerable confessor, Gerberen, for help. The resourceful priest arranged for her escape, accompanied by the king's fool and the fool's wife. The foursome boarded a boat, disguised as a troupe of players, and after some time arrived on the coast of Flanders. They travelled on till they arrived at the village of Gheel, not far from Antwerp. They spent the night in an inn.

The next day, venturing into the woods, they found an oratory dedicated to St Martin. They built a cell there, and lived happily in the service of God.

Still the king pursued his daughter. After a year and a day, some of his retinue arrived in Gheel and took lodgings in the inn. The next day, when they were paying the reckoning, the innkeeper remarked that he had seen similar coins to these before, when a beautiful lady and her companions stayed there. Soon, Dympna was tracked down. The king's men sent for the king.

When the king arrived, he ordered his men to behead Gerberen. Then he proposed to Dympna again; again she refused him. So he ordered his men to behead her; when they hesitated, he cut off her head himself. This double martyrdom, which took place on 30 May 600, was witnessed by the fool and his wife, who were hiding in the woods where they had been foraging for wild herbs. The fool wrote a ballad about the life of Dympna, from which we have her story.

Some centuries later, a woodsman fell asleep under an oak tree. He dreamed that Dympna appeared to him, telling him that he was sleeping on her grave. When the site was excavated, two sarcophagi of white marble were found, in which reposed the bodies of Dympna and Gerberen.

The relics were translated to Gheel. Shortly afterwards, the first miracle was witnessed: a carpenter, fixing the roof of St Dympna's church, accidentally cut off his thumb; when he invoked the name of the saint, the thumb was immediately restored. Not even the trace of a wound remained on his hand.

The next day, a certain woman possessed by an evil spirit was led before the relics of the saint. Within the hour, she vomited several buttons, beads, crooked pins, portions of hair and clots of blood. By midnight, her bodily contortions had ceased, so that she was deemed fit to be released from her chains, and she rapidly regained her former faculties. From then on, any mentally infirm petitioner to Dympna's shrine was likely to be healed; for Dympna's martyrdom was a triumph over her father's insane lust, which is embodied by the demon which accompanies her image.

Curiously, the holy picture I had found on my bed showed a fair-headed Dympna; in my *Lives of the Saints*, her hair was black.

17

OXBLOOD

The question of St Dympna's hair immediately reminded me of the bizarre case of the Red-headed League, and I took out *The Adventures of Sherlock Holmes* from my bedside bookcase to check some of the more salient points of the narrative. Scanning its pages, I saw once more the subject of the story, the down-at-heel pawnbroker Jabez Wilson, costumed in his 'rather baggy grey shepherd's check trousers, a not over-clean black frock-coat, unbuttoned in front, and a drab waistcoat with a heavy brassy Albert chain, with a square pierced bit of metal dangling down as an ornament'. I noted the frayed top-hat and the faded brown overcoat on the chair beside him, and the blazing red head of the man himself. As I relished again the ingenuity of the criminal mind which had created the fictitious League around this other-wise banal feature, there was a knock at the bedroom door.

Uncle Celestine entered. He was wearing his dark green heather-fleck thornproof tweed three-piece suit, a white ray-onized cotton shirt with a faint red stripe, a maroon tie stuck with a gold pin, and tan brogues. He was carrying an oxblood briefcase. It looked as if he meant business: I was used to seeing him in a soft-collared shirt and a Fair Isle sleeveless sweater.

He sat himself down on the bed and looked at me diagnostically. He hoped, he said, that I was keeping all right, and had not been too disturbed by my recent experiences. He had suffered from food-poisoning once himself, and knew of its more bizarre effects. It was important, he said, to put it all down to experience. For even bad can be put to good and, though a burnt child dreads the fire, the child, we must remember, is father to the &c.

He had, said Celestine, been thinking of my further education, now that I was temporarily confined to bed and could not attend school. He noted that I had been doing exceptionally well in Art, and to that effect he had brought me a present which he hoped would assist in my recuperation, for he considered it an example of what I should strive to reproduce.

Painting, he said, is the art of making things real, because you have looked at how things are. In order to paint a twig you must look at a twig, and to paint a tree you must look &c. Only then do you bring the two things together. But you must also remember the injunction of Cennino, that the occupation known as painting requires you to discover things not seen, and present them to the eye as if they actually exist.

I see you are reading Conan Doyle, said Celestine. You will recall the bust of Holmes, by Oscar Meunier of Grenoble, that Holmes had placed in the upstairs front window of 221b Baker Street, in order to deceive the villainous Colonel Moran, formerly of the 1st Bengalore Pioneers, author of *Heavy Game of the*

Western Himalayas, and member of the Bagatelle Card Club, who had determined to shoot Holmes, from a room directly opposite his lodgings, with an air-gun constructed by the blind German mechanic Von Herder, in the story known as 'The Empty House'. Of course, Moran shot the bust of Holmes instead of Holmes. This was an example of art imitating life, or life imitating art, depending on &c.

Uncle Celestine then opened his briefcase and took out a book. It was called *The Van Eycks*.

18

MILK

On the cover of the book was a reproduction of the painting Berenice and I had entered. I stared at it, fascinated.

Ah, the Arnolfini, said Celestine. Since the theory that this painting represents a marriage contract is open to reproach, let us not call it the Arnolfini Wedding, but the Arnolfini Double Portrait. A masterpiece of illusion, is it not? Look how van Eyck has rendered the main figures. Note the textures of the man's dark crimson-purple velvet tabard, or *heuque*, trimmed with sable, over a satin damask doublet worked in arabesques and leaf shapes, grey on black, culminating in the cuffs of silver braid on a purple background, the right cuff tied with a silver-tipped scarlet lace. He wears purple hose and boots. Note the hat: the best hats in the world were made in Bruges.

As for the lady, she wears an elaborately folded, fluted white linen headdress, and fine gold chains around her neck; over an underdress of hyacinth blue damask, whose sleeves are gathered at the wrists into bands of gold and pink braid, an emerald green wool ermine-trimmed gown is gathered up and held across her rounded stomach, so that you might think her pregnant, but she is very definitely not, for van Eyck, in his Dresden triptych of 1437, depicts the virgin St Catherine in similar fashion.

Celestine rapidly flicked through *The Van Eycks* till he came to the relevant plate. There was no doubt about it. The two images were based on the same model, or they were identical twins; they maintained the same pose; and even their gowns, as they fell to the floor, adopted the same folds. In the work of Jan van Eyck, said Celestine, nothing is accidental. We must therefore assume that the history of Catherine of Alexandria was not far from the artist's mind when he painted the Arnolfini Double Portrait.

I have a special devotion to St Catherine myself, admitted Celestine, for she is the patron saint of books. It is said that St Catherine, when pursuing her philosophical studies in the legendary Alexandrian library, was granted a vision of our Lady and the Holy Child, who directed her hand towards a holy book she would not otherwise have opened. By this means she was converted to Christianity, and became its most sophisticated advocate. When the Emperor Maxentius began his persecution, Catherine, still only eighteen years old, rebuked him in person for his tyranny.

Maxentius, failing to answer her arguments against his gods, summoned fifty philosophers to oppose her. After seven days' debate, the philosophers confessed her logic to be irrefutable. They were therefore burned to death by the incensed emperor. Then, overwhelmed by her beauty, he offered her a consort's crown, which she scornfully refused, for she belonged to no earthly king. He commanded her to be torn to bits on a spiked wheel; but this instrument, through angelic intervention, broke asunder, impaling many of the spectators. When she was finally beheaded, milk instead of blood flowed from her severed veins.

As depicted by van Eyck, Catherine holds a sword in one hand; the other grasps an open book, on which is placed a crown.

The Dresden triptych, said Celestine, was painted three years after the Arnolfini Double Portrait; yet when I regard Arnolfini's lady with her hand in his, I cannot help but see the ghost of a sword, a book and a crown. I am confused by time. For time, as St Augustine puts it, is merely an extension: of what, he does not know, until he answers himself, an extension of the mind itself.

19

HYACINTH

Such, as I remember it, was the gist of Celestine's preamble the day he introduced me to van Eyck. I remember the precise date, for I have a letter before me, dated 14 September 1959, the feast of the Exaltation of the Holy Cross, which I received the next morning. The letter was from Berenice:

Dear coz, it read, you will be wondering why you haven't heard from me, because I was wondering about you, and thought you'd be the same. As for me, I'm all right, so perhaps you are too; at least, I will think of you, being well. I don't know if you blame me for what happened. I don't know if I blame myself. Anyway, by now Celestine will have told you he is putting me away to a convent school, in fact, where I'm writing this letter now, it's called St Dympna's and it is run by these Benedictine nuns. It is in the middle of nowhere in the County of Monaghan which is in the Republic. I've only been here a week but already I'm hearing all these stories about it. It is a kind of old dump of a place with lots of corridors and staircases, the dormitories are very bare and the windows have no curtains. Some of the girls say that there is a ghost of an old nun which you see at night if you have to go out to you-know-what, and she appears at the end of the corridor against this barred window, rattling her chains and looking at you from under her wimple. They say you can't see her face and that's the scary thing. But if you see her at all it means you have to become a nun yourself, and then they send you off to this other convent in a place called Gheel, which is near Antwerp in Belgium, to make you into one. County Monaghan is wet even in September, there's a lot of mist does be on the bog. The convent girls call the country girls bog-trotters. I won't say what they call the boys. In fact you hardly see a boy from one day to the next except the cook's son, and he's a half-wit. The food is terrible, porridge with lumps in it and cold toast for breakfast which is at the scrake of dawn, what they call mutton pie for dinner which is at one, and then what they call supper at six – they have the Angelus bonging away before you can even sit down and eat, and then you get more cold toast except with jam if you like, and what they call Shamrock Tea, which is a joke because they say there's only three leaves in it. If only they knew. Then they have this old nun standing up as you eat, and she reads you out a bit of the life of whatever saint's feast day it is; it might be one of them that kissed the lepers' sores one day, and someone that was burned alive another, though the day before yesterday wasn't bad, because it was the feast of St Hyacinth, and it had him shunning the fleshpots of Rome, and all the girls thought he must have been a lovely man. Would you believe it??? There is a copy of the Picture in the Mother Superior's office, I saw it the first day when they brought me in. I got the shivers just looking at it, and they began looking at me funny and asking me if I was all right. Curiouser and curiouser. Otherwise things are OK. I am learning French which should prove useful if I ever have to go to Belgium, ha ha. Must dash as it is almost time for le dreaded souper. Write if you can. As ever —

Berenice.

20

LAPIS LAZULI

My reply is dated 18 September:

> Dear Berenice,
>
> I was pleased to get your letter and I am glad to hear you are keeping well. You are right when you say it is getting curiouser and curiouser because today is the feast of St Joseph of Cupertino, who is the patron saint of flying, as you know. I was also very interested that your nuns are Benedictine, because yesterday was the feast of St Hildegard, who was also a Benedictine nun, and my *Lives of the Saints* says she wrote a book of studies on the elements, plants, trees, minerals, fishes, birds, quadrupeds and reptiles, and another book about the circulation of the blood, headaches, vapours and giddiness, frenzy, insanity, and obsessions.
>
> So I wouldn't be surprised if you got a reading from her life over supper. In fact the 17th of September is also the feast day of St Lambert, so the plot thickens. He is the patron saint

of Liège (pop. 174,000) which is the capital of the Walloon district. Liège has a famous Jesuit college and the largest gun factory in Europe. Uncle Celestine did call in and he told me you had gone away to boarding school. I am keeping all right although my mother makes me drink a cup of Bovril every day, but it's not so bad because I have a whole bottle of Lucozade at my bedside, and I can drink it any time I want.

The other news is that they are sending me away to boarding school too. I am looking forward to it because the boarding schools in stories are always good fun. The school is called Loyola House after St Ignatius of Loyola who founded the Jesuits and it is in County Down beside the Mourne Mountains, so the boys enjoy many outdoor pursuits. I didn't know Uncle Celestine went there, but he tells me it is his alma mater and has produced many famous lawyers and doctors.

Now wait till you hear this. Uncle Celestine has also given me a book which is called *The Van Eycks*. The Picture is in fact by Jan van Eyck who was born in Maastricht. They say that Jan van Eyck had two brothers. One was Lambert! and the other was Hubert, who is called after St Hubert who was bishop of Maastricht! Anyway, the book says the Picture is called the Arnolfini Wedding, though Uncle Celestine thinks that is wrong, because we don't really know if a wedding is going on or not. I think it is a good idea to have this book.

One of the things about the book is that I am getting to know the Picture better and in fact I sometimes dream about it at night, except I'm not scared at all. I like the colours in it very much, and it is interesting because they give you a lot of information about what the colours were made of in those days. For example, the woman's dress is made of verdigris, underpainted with lead-tin yellow and lead white. They also say that some of these colours were poisonous and sometimes artists ended up going mad because of them.

In the dream I don't go into the Picture, I just stare into it. The colours are so deep. I'm starting to see things in it I didn't know were there before. They say that van Eyck had an eye like a microscope. I especially like the blue in the woman's sleeves, which is ultramarine. Van Eyck made this colour from lapis lazuli, a very precious stone. I must dash now as it is time for the dreaded Bovril.

Yours faithfully –

21

PERMANENT BLACK

My letter is written in a careful cursive roundhand on Basildon Bond unlined cream wove notepaper, in Quink Permanent Black ink, manufactured by the Parker Pen Company, of London. I remember the pen I used (a Parker Duofold with a green and black mock tortoiseshell barrel) and the presentation box it came in, together with an accompanying leaflet detailing the product's virtues:

> *A fountain pen, to be perfect, should fulfil certain requirements. It should be of convenient form and size and as light as possible. Its ink-carrying capacity should be as large as is consistent with its portability. It should not be ready to empty itself, except when required to do so, then only at a rate not exceeding the requirements of the writer. It should be prompt in delivering ink the instant the pen touches the paper. It should have as few working parts as possible, and should be free from complication or liability to injure it from careless handling.*

Your Parker Duofold has been designed to meet these
specifications. It is always ready to write — anytime — anywhere. It
never hesitates or splutters or scratches, for the velvet smooth Parker
Duofold point is guaranteed to give 25 years' faithful service, while
the barrel and cap of Parker 'Permanite' are practically
unbreakable.

Parker Pens are Empire Made.

Reading these words, it seemed to me that the Duofold had a mind of its own: the writer, searching for inspiration, had merely to give the pen its head, and it would fill the pages unhesitatingly. It was a view shared by my mother, who had given me the Duofold as a 'recuperation present'. She entertained some ambitions for me as a future writer, and I recognize, in my letter to Berenice, my attempts to follow her advice on correct paragraphing. My mother's side of the family had been brought up to appreciate literature: she was *née* Joyce, and her great-uncle Augustine had achieved a certain distinction in the field. Presentation copies of his works were proudly displayed in the family bookcase.

As it was, I was engrossed in *The Van Eycks*. I thought that if I used my Parker Duofold to copy out some of the text, I might better understand it; or, as if by magic, the words would become mine:

Unlike paints based on egg or water, Eyckian oil paint can be
applied flatly over large areas without leaving brushmarks;
and by changing its consistency or exploiting its slow-drying

properties, it can give a wide range of textural effects. Whether laid down as impasto, or built up in thin glazes, or limned in as a single brush-stroke, oil paint can produce the utmost clarity of colour. Before the viewer's eyes, a typical van Eyck shimmers, as if composed of overlapping, full colour stereoscopic slides. It is like being hypnotized by precious stones, or gazing into luminous, deep water. Van Eyck duplicated with the brush the work of goldsmiths in metal and gems, recapturing that glow which seemed to reflect the radiance of the Divine, the superessential light. For viewed in that eternal light, all things are equal, from the glint of a nail in the wooden floor of a burgher's house, to the glittering spires of the New Jerusalem.

22

DELFT BLUE

Under each of these entries I wrote the date, and some notes on the life of the saint whose feast it was. Thus, under the entry cited above, I find:

19 September: St Januarius. The standing miracle, as it is called by Baronius, of the blood of St Januarius liquefying and boiling up at the approach of the martyr's head is renowned throughout Christendom. In a rich chapel, called the Treasury, in the great church at Naples, are preserved the blood, in two very old glass vials, and the head of St Januarius. The blood is congealed, and of a dark colour; but when brought in sight of the head, though at a considerable distance, it melts, bubbles up and, upon the least motion, flows on any side. It happens equally in all seasons of the year, and in a variety of circumstances. The usual times when it is performed are the feast of St Januarius, the 19th of September; that of the translation of his relics, the Sunday

which falls next to the calends of May; and the 20th of December, on which day, in 1631, a terrible eruption of Mount Vesuvius was extinguished, and the flow of boiling lava halted in its tracks, upon invoking the patronage of this martyr.

Somehow, as I wrote these words, I could not help but visualize the reservoir of my Duofold as a kind of rubber reliquary, holding ink instead of blood; but I banished this thought by remarking how lucky I was to live in an island bereft of volcanic activity and blessed with an equable climate. That September, indeed, was especially mild, though with a touch of frost at nights; by day the air was clarified, the skies a Delft blue.

As I leafed through *The Van Eycks*, I began to see how the skies of Jan van Eyck resembled ours. The same distances, looking newly washed by rain. The same framing from interiors, as I could see my sky framed by the sick-bay window, and the spires and walls of the city beyond. The same equilibrium of birds poised in the sky above the figures stilled in civic squares, dealing with unworldly peace. I thought of Chinese landscapes on blue Delftware.

On 21 September, the feast of St Matthew the Evangelist, who is usually represented sitting at his desk, writing, with an angel either guiding his hand or holding the inkwell, I came across a reference to Gheel in *The Van Eycks*; I remembered Berenice had mentioned this place in her letter.

Gheel is a town of some 14,600 inhabitants, near Antwerp,

which derives its principal interest from the colony of
lunatics established there and in the neighbouring villages.
The patients are boarded out among the peasants, whose
labours and domestic pursuits they share, and they are
permitted to walk about without restraint within the limits
of their district. This excellent and humane system has
always been attended with favourable results: so much so
that the casual visitor will sometimes find it hard to
distinguish by their demeanour between those who are mad
and those who are not. Any treatise dealing with the work of
the van Eycks would be remiss if it were not to mention that
in Gheel, at the shrine of St Dympna, in the church of her
name, there is a small icon (6¾ × 3½″) of St Barbara,
reverenced by the Gheelois as being the work of Jan van
Eyck. However, independent experts have concluded that
the oak panel on which the Gheel Barbara is painted can date
no earlier than the 16th century; that the brushwork has
been executed by a left-handed person; and that van Eyck's
alleged signature, in the sky above the tower which is St
Barbara's attribute, is the work of an 18th century
ecclesiastical hand. In other words, the Gheel Barbara is an
excellent, if well-intentioned forgery, and we need treat of it
no further.

23

BELLADONNA

Being an extract from *A Pilgrim in Flanders*, by J. Augustine Joyce, author of *Rambles in the Dordogne*, *A Wanderer in Venice*, *Rome Revisited*, *The Holy Places of Jerusalem*, etc., Sheed & Ward, London, 1892.

By starting out at an early yet suitable hour from the metropolis of Antwerp, the morning train will leave the traveller at Herenthals station. There, a well-appointed omnibus will be found, waiting to receive its contingent of passengers, baggage, and mail packets, destined for the quaint old city of Gheel. Off at a spanking pace start the vigorous roadsters, over the paved highway, under long and regular lines of oak and elm. At various intervals, signposts mark the direction and distances of neighbouring cities by kilometres; and before long, the traveller finds himself disembarking in the ancient centre of Gheel. He will do well to install himself in the quaint-looking, but excellent inn –

L'Hôtel de l'Agneau – with the sign of the stork in front, in the market square, just opposite St Dympna's church. Bed and board may be obtained for four Belgian francs.

In the course of a discursive ramble through the old Flemish streets, the traveller will not fail to notice the perfume which breathes from the extensive herb-gardens, which are harvested in their due seasons to provide physic for the colony of lunatics established in Gheel and its environs. Here are grown, among others, Aconite, St John's Wort, Valerian, Belladonna, Pennyroyal, Balm, and Jessamine. It is a tradition among the Gheelois that the receipt for the celebrated Gheel remedy has been transmitted orally from the very jester who accompanied St Dympna on her flight from Ireland, for it is said that he discovered the therapeutic properties of certain plants while foraging the vicinity of St Martin's oratory, where Dympna and her retinue found refuge.

Nor should the traveller be surprised to hear music in the streets, for this too is considered a therapy. The Irish pilgrim in particular will be pleased to detect a peculiarly Celtic, almost harp-like strain in the tuneful Flemish bagpipe, which the Gheelois attribute to the influence of the jester, who is reported to have been proficient on Ireland's national instrument.

After these enjoyable interludes, the traveller should then repair to St Dympna's church itself, for it is a powerful and evocative store-room of images. At the right entrance to the great choir is a beautiful statue of the saint, in an alcove, covered with a bulletproof glass case. Under an emerald silk robe she wears an elegant white dress trimmed with lace cuffs and collars, for lace-making is an important cottage industry in Gheel. A rich lace scarf falls from the elegant silk mantilla, and a brass basin rests before the image, to receive the offerings of Dympna's faithful clients.

The high altar and its superstructure, within the great choir, provide truly majestic and elaborate specimens of sculpture, divided into many compartments, each depicting significant moments in the life of the saint. They form a veritable mine of illustration, and the pilgrim is advised to spend some days studying this iconography, committing it to memory. It is helpful, in one's meditations, to think of each image, or station, as a drawer in an extensive cabinet: for then one can, in the future, mentally open each compartment to reveal its contents, and contemplate their inner meaning. Thus the past and future meet, in the eternal present of St Dympna's shrine.

24

BERYL

According to the Revd Joyce, the Gheelois maintain an elaborate
tradition regarding the icon of St Barbara; and, while allowing that
some embellishment has occurred over the centuries, he is inclined
to trust in the essentials of the story, which goes more or less as follows, for I have considerably abridged his exhaustive account:

On St Mark's Day, 25 May 1421, a man of about thirty appeared
outside the apothecary's shop in Gheel. He was dressed in the
highest fashion of the time, though one of his wooden overshoes
was missing, and he was hatless. He was soaking wet, and obvi-
ously in some distress. When approached and questioned, he
could not tell by what means he had got there; nor did he know
his name. He remembered standing by the banks of a canal in a
great city, examining the reflection of a church tower in the
waters, when it was struck by a great ball of fire and disintegrated
in a blinding flash of light. He knew no more. When he came to,
he found himself where he was.

The Gheelois were not unduly perturbed by this apparition, for the stranger's brief story was no more fantastic than others they had heard. Though bereft of a past, the man seemed intelligent. He was christened Marcus, and taken in by the apothecary, Dr Bredius, who put him to work at menial tasks in the shop. He soon displayed a remarkable predilection for medicine, and within weeks had absorbed the contents of Dr Bredius's library. In his spare time he was seen to forage the nearby woods and pastures, meticulously examining the plant life. Within a few weeks, Dr Bredius allowed him unlimited access to his laboratory.

On 27 July, the feast of the Seven Sleepers of Ephesus, Marcus was scrutinizing the pages of a newly illustrated herbal proudly shown to him by Bredius. Suddenly, he hurled the expensive volume at the wall.

Useless! he cried, they are all useless! These illustrators have no eyes! They portray what they believe, not what they see!

With that, he collapsed into a chair; when he had recovered himself, he begged Bredius to forgive him the damage to his book. He would, he promised, recompense him a hundred times over by making him a herbal that would show the actuality of plants, instead of the stereotypes which prevailed at the time.

He set to work. On Bredius's recommendation he obtained a set of artist's materials and a beryl magnifying stone. Now he was abroad in the countryside more than ever, looking closer and closer into things, noting their attributes in a little book. Flowers had as many colours as their surfaces and facets. He ran out of names for them. Now he spent many hours in the laboratory, for he knew his paints could never register this glazed, layered clarity: traditional tempura was too thick. He wanted the inner light to shine through. Eventually, he hit on a volatile oil distilled from the resin of the terebinth tree, hence called turpentine: dissolved in this medium, his colours could achieve a thinner than gossamer film.

On 18 October 1421 – appropriately, it was the feast of St Luke, patron of artists – Marcus presented Dr Bredius with the beautifully illustrated volume he had promised. On 4 December, the feast of St Barbara, a thunderbolt struck the apothecary's shop. Within seconds, it became an inferno, fuelled by the shop's stock of volatile chemicals. By some miracle, the blaze confined itself to the premises, and the adjoining buildings were left unscathed. The charred remains of Dr Bredius were discovered the next morning; but of Marcus, and his marvellous book, there was no sign, nor were they ever seen again.

25

SMOKE

That same morning – 5 December, the feast of St Sabas, who, as a hermit, shared a cave with a lion – the sacristan of St Dympna's church found, among the votive offerings at her shrine, an oak panel bearing a small painting of St Barbara. My book of saints had this to say about St Barbara:

During the reign of Maximian, there lived a rich pagan, Dioscorus, who had an only daughter, Barbara. She was so beautiful that he had her confined to a high tower. Nevertheless, her hand was sought by numerous princes. Dioscorus was impatient for her to choose between them, but Barbara refused to be married.

One day, when Dioscorus was away on business, she escaped from her tower and came across some workmen who were building a new bathhouse for her father's palace. When she saw that the men had only planned for two windows, she commanded them to put in a third. Just then, a holy man passed by, who baptized her in the waters of the bathhouse.

When her father returned, he demanded to know why three windows should give better light than two. Barbara pointed out that this was clearly an emblem of the Trinity, and of the divine light which informs all things. The pagan father, enraged, drew his sword; but Barbara miraculously flew out the window, and landed on a distant mountain. Dioscorus pursued her and, taking her by the hair, shut her up again in the tower. When, after torture, she refused to submit to his pagan gods, he led her up the mountain, where he cut off her head. As he was returning to his palace, a thunderbolt descended from Heaven, and burned him to a cinder.

Conventionally, Barbara is depicted holding a miniature tower in one hand, and a martyr's palm in the other. The painter of the Gheel icon chose to make the tower an even more dominant feature of the composition than the saint herself, who is seated before it, bearing her palm. The perspective is such that the tower, in which there is a great tripartite window, appears several hundreds of feet high. This treatment corresponds closely with that of the St Barbara in the Musée Royal des Beaux-Arts in Antwerp, which bears the inscription *IOH(ann)ES DE EYCK ME FECIT (Jan van Eyck made me) 1437*. As in the Gheel Barbara, the elaborate Gothic tower in the Antwerp image is still under construction, suggesting the tower of Babel. It is thus a figure of hubris and incomprehension; and elements of its architecture have been compared to those of the great Belfry of Bruges, which was wrecked by lightning three times in its history.

In the foreground of the Gheel icon is a great profusion of

flowers and herbs, rendered in botanically identifiable detail; today, they are somewhat obscured by the candle smoke and incense of centuries, but to the people of Gheel, some five hundred years ago, they must have seemed miraculously real; and it was plain to all that the St Barbara could be the work of none other than the apothecary's apprentice, Marcus, who had so mysteriously appeared and vanished from their lives. Written in the sky above the tower were the words *Johann de eyck fuit hic (Jan van Eyck has been here) 1421*; from which it was concluded that Jan van Eyck and Marcus were one and the same man.

26

VENETIAN RED

My recuperation passed quite pleasantly, between reading, copying out what I had read, and studying the plates in *The Van Eycks*. I learned that little was known about Lambert van Eyck beyond his name, and that some historians considered the existence of Hubert to be problematic, all of which added to the allure of their brother Jan – John of Oak, once thought to be from Maaseyck, the Oak on the Maas, but since shown to be born in Maastricht, further down the river. Van Eyck executed pictures on oak panels, in which things were painted to imitate carved oak; and in the Arnolfini Double Portrait, there is a trinity of carved figurines whose relationship is hard to figure out.

They are St Margaret and her dragon on the back of the chair; a squatting lion on the arm of the same chair; and a grotesque perched on the arm of the settle, depicting a beast back-to-back with its mirror image. Van Eyck's wife's name was Margaret; St Margaret had emerged from the belly of a dragon. The lion was the emblem of St Mark, but also of Jerome, author of the

Vulgate, and patron saint of learning, who pulled a thorn from a lion's paw and thus domesticated him. As to what the grotesque stood for, I did not know; but I did know that it had been deemed appropriate for me to depart for Loyola House on 30 September, the feast of St Jerome.

When I woke up that morning, an austere light flowed through the window, illuminating the folds of my Loyola House uniform arranged on a hanger on the bedroom door: the navy blue blazer over the crisp white shirt, draped with the Oxford Blue tie striped with Cambridge Blue; the charcoal grey trousers. Black Oxford shoes rested on the floor. As I donned the immaculate ensemble, I felt myself becoming another person. Gone was the boy; I was now a growing man. As I knotted my tie in the wardrobe mirror, I briefly saw a stranger.

My mother had made a great breakfast whose sausages and bacon glistened as she transferred them from the pan to my gleaming plate. Tendrils of aroma rose from the tea and the fry. The butter looked buttercup yellow, the sugar-bowl was filled with cubes of snowy light. The burst yolk of my egg oozed over the white. As I mopped it up with a forkful of white bread my mother took out a little pill-box from her overall, and opened it to show me a square of linen faintly stained with what looked like rust.

It was, she said, a relic of Fra Angelico, the patron saint of painters, bequeathed to her by her great-uncle Joyce, who had procured it, at some expense, after much negotiation, from a dealer in such items at a stall outside St Mark's in Venice, in which church Fra Angelico is known to have worked; and she was confident its power would stand me in good stead in my studies. It had, indeed, inspired her great-uncle, who freely admitted that the more lyrical passages of his best-known book, *A Pilgrim in Flanders*, were almost entirely due to its influence.

A horn sounded. My uncle Celestine's car – a black Morris Oxford – was at the door. I packed my belongings, kissed my mother farewell, and got in. I had never been driven much before and I was looking forward to the journey. My uncle Celestine lit a pipe. When it was drawing to his satisfaction, he drove off. Now, my boy, he said, now that we're together for a while, we can have a good long chat.

I settled down to listen to him.

27

FORGET-ME-NOT

I thought, said Celestine, that it might be proper for me to out-line the life of St Ignatius of Loyola, but I am sure you are already familiar with its salient features, and no doubt the good fathers of Loyola House will educate you further with regard to St Ignatius in due course. It occurred to me, instead, to relate an anecdote of my brief relationship with the philosopher Ludwig Wittgenstein, who worked as an under-gardener at Loyola House in the spring of 1949. I was an assistant teacher at the time; I confess it was only two years afterwards – when I read an obituary of Wittgenstein, who died on 29 April 1951, the feast of St Catherine of Siena – that I realized how celebrated he was.

That spring of '49, I had often seen Wittgenstein about his work in the garden or in the large heated conservatory, and had occasionally engaged him in trivial conversation about the weather, or related matters. On 26 April, however, things took a more meaningful turn. That evening, wine was served with dinner, and Wittgenstein, who normally took his meals in the servants' quarters, was present at the table. Upon further enquiry I learned that it was his sixtieth birthday, and the good fathers, who I now suppose had some inkling of his status in the world of philosophy, had deemed it appropriate to celebrate the occasion in the above manner.

I took the opportunity to examine his person carefully. He was slightly built, but very neat and compact, about five feet six inches in height, with tanned, aquiline features, piercing blue eyes, and a shock of curly brown hair going grey at the temples. One would have taken him for a sprightly fifty. He wore a pair of flannel trousers, a flannel shirt open at the throat, and a leather jacket; this, I was to learn later, was his notion of formal dress. He was very clean, and his brown shoes had been recently polished. Although he appeared somewhat taciturn, he had a singular presence. When eating, he kept his head down, approaching only one component of his meal at a time: first the peas, then the carrots, and finally the potatoes; he did not touch the meat, nor did he take any wine, but drank copious amounts of water.

When he had finished, he was rising to leave the table when I happened to draw his attention to the nice coincidence that his birthday fell on the feast day of the third pope, St Cletus. His forget-me-not blue eyes turned towards me; he sat down and poured a glass of water. You know Cletus? he said. More correctly known as Anacletus?

I replied that I had been christened Celestine, after Pope Celestine V, and was tolerably familiar with the papal succession.

Ah, Celestine, he said, the patron of bookbinders. You know, of course, that the existence of Anacletus has been called into question, since the name is a Greek adjective meaning 'blame-less'; and St Paul, in his epistle to Titus, stipulated that a bishop should be *blameless — not given to wine, not given to filthy lucre; holding fast to the faithful word*. So his doubters think Anacletus to be a verbal construct. An interesting enigma, is it not?

For language is full of traps, continued Wittgenstein, and *there are many unruly and vain talkers and deceivers*. Indeed, if my memory serves me, Paul goes on to cite the paradox of the Cretan liar: *One of themselves, even a prophet of their own, said, the Cretans are always liars*.

Wittgenstein bowed formally, and left me with this remark: *On the other hand, everything that can be said can be said clearly.*

28

VERMILION

Over the next few weeks, said Celestine, Wittgenstein and I became more familiar. I learned that his position as gardener was purely honorary, for he did not receive payment for his services. He liked, he said, to do gardening from time to time, as a respite from his other work, which was 'doing philosophy'; I was unsure as to whether this was a pastime or an occupation. He had first done gardening in 1920, with the monks at Hütteldorf in Vienna, some time after his release from the prisoner-of-war camp at the great Benedictine abbey of Monte Cassino: I then gathered that, as an Austrian, he had fought on the German side.

To work with growing things is good for the soul, he said in his faultless English. It enables one to dream.

He told me then of a dream he had had in the winter of 1919, when he was still imprisoned.

It was night, and very cold. I was outside a house whose windows blazed with light. I went up to a window to look inside. There, on the floor, I noticed an exquisitely beautiful prayer rug, one which I immediately wanted to examine. I tried to open the front door, but a snake darted out to prevent me from entering. I tried another door, but there, too, a snake darted out to block my way. Snakes appeared also at the windows and blocked my every effort to reach the prayer rug. Then I woke up.

When Wittgenstein asked me what I thought this dream might mean, I enquired if he could remember its precise date. He could not be clear, but thought it might have been early November. Could it have been the 3rd? I asked. He thought that such a date was quite possible; I then pointed out that 3 November was the feast day of the Spanish bishop, St Pirmin, who is invoked against snakes, because, having escaped the Moorish persecution, he found himself on the island of Reichenau, from which he expelled the serpents. Thereafter he established the first monastery on German soil. These events, it seemed to me, were clearly linked to Wittgenstein's dream, and I offered a possible interpretation, as follows:

The house blazing with light is the monastery of Reichenau; the prayer rug, its inner sanctum; either that, or it is a Moorish rug. The snakes are offspring of the devil, who try to prevent access to the house of prayer; either that, or they are Moorish swords. Pirmin is Wittgenstein, fleeing from the war, and finding refuge in the camp below the walls of Monte Cassino, whose windows blaze with light; either that, or Pirmin is St Patrick.

This is most interesting, said Wittgenstein, do go on. I admitted that that was as far as my interpretation went. Then, said Wittgenstein, let me relate to you a kindred dream, which might shed some light on the matter. In early December of 1920 – I cannot remember the precise date, lest you stop and ask me — I dreamt I was a priest. In the front hall of my house there was an altar; to the right of the altar a stairway led off. It was a grand stairway, carpeted in Venetian Red, the red of St John's Blood, rather like that at my former home, the Palais Wittgenstein at the Alleegasse in Vienna. At the foot of the altar, and partly covering it, was an oriental carpet. Several other religious objects and regalia were placed on and beside the altar. One of these was a rod of precious metal.

Here, Wittgenstein paused to gather his thoughts.

29

FIRMAMENT

But a theft occurred, continued Wittgenstein. A thief entered from the left and stole the rod. This event had to be reported to the police, who sent a representative who wanted a description of the rod. For instance, of what sort of metal was it made? I could not say; I could not even say whether it was of silver or of gold. The police officer questioned whether the rod had ever existed in the first place. I then began to examine the other parts and fittings of the altar and noticed that the carpet was a prayer rug. My eyes began to focus on the border of the rug. It was of the blue tint known to colourists as firmament, and made a striking contrast with the beautiful vermilion centre. The more I gazed into the rug, the more it glowed and invited me in. I cannot remember if then I awoke or not. What, said Wittgenstein, do you think this dream means?

I replied that I understood the carpet was sometimes interpreted as an emblem of the garden, for in its patterns may be seen real or mythical flowers, trees, beasts and birds, and since the

medium does not allow too realistic a copy, the formal charac-
teristics displayed by the carpet are those of a garden of the mind.
As for the rod, I did not wish to point out the obvious parallel
with Moses' rod, which changed itself from rod to serpent and
from serpent to rod; in fact, it might well be a gardening tool. I
reminded him that the emblem of St Fiacre, patron of gardeners,
and of cab-drivers, was a staff or rod, with which he miraculously
turned up more soil in a day than he would have done had he used
a horse and plough.

Furthermore, the rod might well be a pilgrim's staff, for Fiacre
was one of many Irish saints whose peregrinations took them all
over Europe: I thought especially of St Gall, patron of birds,
cuckoo-clocks, and Switzerland, who exorcised a girl of an evil
spirit, which flew out of her mouth in the form of a blackbird.
Nor was Dympna, patron saint of those possessed by demons, far
from my mind; indeed, today, 15 May, was her feast. As for
Wittgenstein, he too might be a pilgrim; certainly, he was an
exile.

Wittgenstein nodded thoughtfully. It is true, he said, that I
have sometimes wished myself to be a member of no nation. And
there have been times when I have felt I was not far from madness;
you will not, perhaps, be surprised when I tell you that once I also
gardened in the town of Gheel, where, as you know, St Dympna's
shrine is situated. I was especially interested in the Gheelois
method of cultivating herbs, which form an important part of
their mental patients' regimen. Moreover, I wished to study a
system of government which places little or no physical restraint
on those under its care, but trusts instead to the invisible bonds of

society. I had been in Gheel only a day or two when, accompanied by a physician, I met in one of the public roads a once dangerous maniac, who lived in a cottage at some distance, then carrying an infant in his arms like any nurse. He seemed to take great care of his innocent charge; and the physician remarked that such an occupation constituted this lunatic's chief enjoyment.

In like wise, I observed men and women, happily spinning, weaving or knitting by the firesides, conversing amiably with their hosts, or drinking and smoking in the cabarets of Gheel; so that I had often to enquire, which of them were designated mad and which were sane.

Let me give you some further impressions of my stay at Gheel.

30

COFFEE

As you know, said Wittgenstein, for centuries the people of
Gheel had extended their own families to include all those who
came to them for succour. This relationship was formalized by a
Legislative Act of 18 June 1850, the feast day of the twin martyrs, Mark and Marcellian, and, incidentally, the commemoration
of the Battle of Waterloo. By this Act, every house in which one
or more lunatics resided was considered an insane institution. It
is a system which works to the mutual benefit of all concerned.
The Kempenland, where Gheel is situated, was formerly so
remote and dreary a district, consisting mostly of wild marshes
and dark pine woods, that it was known as the Siberia of the Low
Countries.

Now, driving from Herenthals to Gheel, one cannot but be
impressed by the neatly trimmed hedgerows along the roadside.
White cottages with their red-tiled roofs gleam under the pleasant sun, amid the crops of wheat, oats, beets, swedes, potatoes
and peas. From morn to dewy eve, the moving human figures of

all ages and both sexes, through the neat fields, proclaim the tireless industry of the Kempenlanders, who attribute this transformation of their landscape to the example of the lunatics under their care. These children of God, they say, given comparative liberty, taught them to appreciate the open air, the feel of the earth between their fingers, and the miracle of growing things.

The people of Gheel are mild, and equably disposed. They take people as they come, for they have witnessed all kinds of behaviour. They appreciate story-telling and music-making, and enter willingly into games of make-believe; many of their charges are gifted exponents of these arts. I myself saw, in an enclosed garden adjoining the cottage where he was resident, an imaginary Napoleon – a little man – vociferating and bawling to troops he then believed to be passing under review, ordering Marshal A. and General B., etc., to manoeuvre according to imperial command. Within minutes, a troupe of children, armed with brooms and walking-sticks, arrived on the scene: the emperor's eyes lit up; and the campaign thus continued for some hours, ending only when the emperor commanded one of his little aides to bring him to his tent, for he had had enough of battle for one day.

I was also introduced to a Sherlock Holmes who, after we had exchanged pleasantries for some minutes, asked me how things were in my native Vienna, for it must be greatly changed since the war. When I expressed some astonishment at how he could have known my point of origin, he spoke as follows:

As you came into the room accompanied by the doctor, you were whistling the tune of Franz Schubert's song, 'The Wanderer', which is very popular among citizens of Vienna, especially when they are far from home. A fine rendition, I might add. Then, when you sat down to the refreshments kindly supplied by Mrs Hudson, you dunked your biscuit into your coffee in a peculiarly Viennese manner. These inferences by themselves were not conclusive, but when I observed that your jacket has five buttons on the cuff, rather than the customary two or three, or the four favoured by Savile Row in London, I was certain that you were from Vienna, for only in Vienna do the tailors insist on five-button cuffs. That you speak French with a refined Viennese accent is immaterial, for it is often affected by persons who aspire to a culture they do not possess.

Of even more interest than the imaginary Holmes, however, was the man known as Dioscorides.

31

SHAMROCK

Dioscorides believed himself to be a reincarnation of Dioscorides, the Greek physician acknowledged as the author of the first pharmacopoeia, thought to have been published in AD 77. His account of some 600 medicinal herbs was supplemented by the earlier work of Crateuas, endorsed by Pliny as the originator of botanical illustration; and this compilation was regarded as a holy writ of medicine even as late as the Renaissance. However, as Dioscorides was repeatedly copied, the manuscripts accumulated errors, and the illustrations in particular – however accurate they might have been in the first century BC – degenerated into increasingly fictitious figures, which not only failed to resemble the plants depicted, but also incorporated mythological notions of their origins and attributes.

The Gheel Dioscorides, who in his previous life had been an illustrator of medical textbooks, was familiar with this history; and from the moment it was revealed to him that he was indeed Dioscorides, he had set about compiling an illustrated herbal that would truly hold the mirror up to nature and be received as the authority on the matter for all time. It was for this express purpose that he had come to Gheel and made himself resident there, since the herb gardens of Gheel were renowned throughout Europe, and afforded a perfect field for study.

Dioscorides was a person of some note in Gheel. Tall, in his late sixties, with a mane of white hair and a full white beard, he was always immaculately dressed, usually in a bespoke Prince of Wales check suit, a wideawake hat and, when the weather demanded it, a cape. He was never without his walking-stick, which was carved in the figure of a snake coiled around a staff: this was the attribute of Asclepius, the Greek god of medicine, because the snake, when it sloughs its skin, renews itself. Popular with ladies of a certain age, he was nonetheless respected by professional men, and was well thought of even by the clergy. His reputation for treating morbid conditions which had eluded conventional treatment was second to none.

I had occasion to experience one of Dioscorides' remedies myself when I was smitten by one of my periodic fits of nervous debilitation. One day, I felt under an almost palpable cloud. I was kneeling on the crazy paving between parterres, tending a plot of elecampane, when I heard the oncoming tip-tap of a stick. I looked up: it was Dioscorides.

You look pale, young man, he said, as he rocked on his heels with his thumbs in his fob pockets. You need a remedy. You are Austrian, are you not? In your Alps are to be found many flora beneficial for one in your condition. Transplanted to Gheel, they have undergone a sea change. Some failed to take at first, but the lunatic gardeners appealed to their flexible natures; before long, a new strain – something rich and strange – emerged and flourished under Belgian conditions. What I am about to give you is based on such herbs, supplemented by modicums of some others: I will mention only shamrock, a much underestimated restorative, for it cleanses the doors of perception, and wards off lightning. I have established that the king's fool who accompanied Dympna on her flight from Ireland employed shamrock in his vain attempt to bring her back to life; but it was afterwards found to have a significant effect on the horrified bystanders.

He extracted a little tin vestas box from his fob pocket and handed it to me. It can be smoked in a pipe, or drunk as tea, he said. The effects are quicker when smoked, but when drunk are more lingering. Take it three times a day for one day, and then visit St Dympna's shrine. Then tell me what you see.

32

CARNELIAN

When I woke up the next morning, continued Wittgenstein, I took the first dose in the form of smoke, and went down for breakfast in the under-gardeners' refectory. Here, on a long deal table, were arrayed the typical constituents of a Belgian buffet: sliced cheeses, sausages and hams, peeled hardboiled eggs, four kinds of bread, butter, jams, coffee. My appetite at such an hour is small, and is customarily satisfied with a piece of rye bread and a café au lait, yet never had the menu appeared so enticing: for the first time I noticed how convoluted were the curls of butter in their scallop dishes, the blue sheen in the whites of the boiled eggs. The cheeses glowed with different yellows. The bread was flecked with many grains and smelt of yeast. Wisps of coffee roast were in the air. I will not speak about the sausages and hams, but the jams shone like precious stones: the raspberry, in particular, like carnelian.

It was as if the world till then had been marginally blurred, and now shimmered into focus. Every thing beheld its proper, self-sufficient space. I knew I had never looked at anything properly before. You will recall the passage in St Augustine's *Confessions*, where he speaks of how he learned to talk:

I noticed that my elders would name some object, he says, and then turn towards whatever it was they had named. I watched them and understood that the sound they made when they wanted to indicate that particular thing was the name which they gave to it.

And so he goes on. It is a description I admire deeply, but what is to happen when you run out of names? To return to the sausages, how can we describe the different archipelagos of fat in their flat slices; what do we call that cut of pink, that salami red? What do we know about the work of a charcutier? One sausage alone is a very deep subject.

I helped myself to a feast as I had never done before. When I had eaten my fill, I went out into the garden about my work. This proved difficult: whereas before, I knew each herb by its generic name, now I could see only specific plants; not only that, but each leaf of them required my individual attention. Then there were details of the leaves I found impossible to contemplate for any time, for each led me on to a different configuration. Green was not green, but innumerable greens.

By lunchtime I had done no work as such, but felt I had travelled many miles. I realized that to follow every crack of the crazy paving would take a snail many centuries, as the ants traversed universes. I decided then to have no lunch, but go for a stroll around down-town Gheel instead. Music wafted from the cabarets, above the hum of conversation and the clink of cutlery and glasses; but I only wanted to be alone.

I travelled to the outskirts, and sat down in a field. By now, I should have taken the second dose of Dioscorides' remedy. Luckily, I had the tin box still in my pocket. I walked into a convenient farmhouse – the door was unlocked – and asked the farmer's wife for a pot of boiling water. She kindly obliged. An elegant plume of steam appeared from the kettle. We made some tea, and drank it. After some hours I felt the need to leave.

Back in Gheel again, I smoked the third dose. The evening Angelus was ringing as I made my way to St Dympna's church.

33

REDCOAT RED

The principal altar of St Dympna's shrine shows a larger than life figure of the saint, elevated on a cloud, surrounded by groups of lunatics, all large statues, whose feet and hands are bound in golden chains, as they had been by iron in bygone days. In a side chapel is an elaborate carving of oak, in eight iconic compartments, thus: her birth; her mother's death; the devil tempting her father; Dympna, Gerberen, the king's fool, and the fool's wife embarking on a ship; the king in pursuit; the king cutting off his daughter's head close to the decapitated corpse of Gerberen; priests carrying her relics; and finally, the devil emerging from the head of a female lunatic. These are stations in the journey of St Dympna through her life and death.

The twelfth gong of the Angelus was still shivering the air as I knelt down to examine this narrative. I was particularly fascinated by Gerberen's head, which, detached from its body, seemed to be looking at me with a quizzical expression. I felt a breeze come as if from nowhere, and the banks of candles before the shrine began to flicker and gutter. They smelled of gunsmoke. Suddenly, I was back in the war, in spring 1916, a soldier in the Austrian Seventh Army, stationed at the southernmost point of the Eastern Front, near the Romanian border. I wanted more than anything to be in the line of fire, for I hoped that the nearness of death would bring me the light of life. I was full of joy when I was assigned to that most dangerous of places, the observation post. I felt like the prince of an enchanted castle.

On 29 April, I was shot at several times. The wind of a bullet fanned my cheek; I felt terror and pity. I learned later that this was the last day of the Easter Uprising in Dublin. It was also the feast of St Catherine of Siena, who is invoked against fire. So, through the grace of God, I survived.

Again I felt the wind on my cheek. My vision was blinded by candle smoke. When it cleared, I was no longer in Gheel, but standing in a field of mud. It was pouring with rain. I saw a series of flashes, and, a split-second later, heard a low, reverberating boom. This was not thunder, I realized, but cannon-fire. A train of horse-drawn carriages lurched by. Again the cannons sounded, and now I could see vast, urgent movements in the landscape. Muffled screams and whoops came from all sides. Some horse soldiers in scarlet jackets galloped out of a wood and surrounded one of the carriages, an elegant vehicle painted a deep blue. They dragged its driver from his perch and cut off his head.

I was powerless to move. The soldiers proceeded to loot the vehicle. Their primary concern, it seemed, was liquor, and they soon discovered some cases, which they set upon with oaths and cries of joy. One of them then emerged from the door of the coach with a strange trophy: a parrot in a cage. It was a bizarre sight: the cursing soldiers in their mud-streaked scarlet jackets, the squawking parrot in his magnificent green, yellow and vermilion.

Vittoria! they shouted, and one of them took a bottle of wine, cut off its neck with his sword, and poured it over the parrot's head. I hereby christen you Vittoria! he cried.

They all fell down in mock obeisance. Then one of them caught sight of me. He raised his pistol and fired. I saw the flash, then felt the bullet penetrate my heart.

When I opened my eyes, I was back in Gheel, but I realized I had been present at the battle of Vittoria, in Spain, in 1813, where Joseph Bonaparte's army had been utterly routed by the British–Portuguese alliance.

34

EMERALD

But here, said Celestine, we must leave Wittgenstein; for we have almost arrived at our destination: Loyola House, 1959.

Indeed, I had been so wrapped up in my uncle's story – and that of Wittgenstein – that I had not noticed the miles go by; nor had time seemed to matter. A whole countryside had slipped by without my seeing it; it had grown dark. It was still the feast day of St Jerome, as it had been when we set off, yet it seemed as if years had passed.

I rubbed my eyes. At the end of the tunnel of light broadcast by the Morris Oxford's headlamps, I caught my first glimpse of Loyola House: gothic turrets swaying amid dark trees, the glint of a neo-classical façade. The car came to a halt on a sweep of gravel. We were met at the postern gate by a porter. Before long I had been taken up a flight of stairs to a room in which sat a Jesuit priest and a boy about my own age. The priest gestured to make ourselves comfortable, and when we were, he began:

I am Fr Brown. This – he nodded towards the boy – is Mr Maeterlinck. You are welcome to Loyola House, where you will be fellows. So, Messrs Maeterlinck and Carson, it is part of my pleasant duty to relate to you, as new pupils, the life of Loyola, which saint has given our establishment his name.

The founder of the Company of Jesus was born Iñigo de Beltran Yañez de Oñaz y Loyola on an unknown date. On 20 May 1521, as the French besieged Pamplona, Loyola, a captain in the army of Navarre, had his right leg shattered by a cannonball. Whilst recuperating, he commanded a book of romances to be brought to him to pass the time; but all that could be found in the castle of Loyola was a life of Christ, and a copy of *The Golden Legend*. This latter compilation was an inspiration to him, for in it the lives of the saints were told like those of soldiers, who held to their cause in spite of dungeon, fire and sword.

Loyola was not an intellectual, nor a metaphysician. He possessed one faculty in abundance: a vivid imagination, in which whatever he conceived assumed a concrete form. When he read, he could see the persons and events described; and his daydreams were realities. One fancy, indulged in for hours at a time, concerned a lovely lady, a queen or empress of some country he would serve. He would ride a white horse, his scarlet doublet contrasting nicely with the green of her gown. In this fashion, he lay on his couch, his vagabond fancies wandering between vanity and religion.

Loyola's leg had to be reset twice. Although it was stretched for days on a rack, it ended up shorter than the left, and he had a limp for the rest of his life. In his delirium, he perceived a strange, monstrous, yet beautiful thing in the form of a serpent, studded with innumerable eyes like emeralds. This vision brought him great comfort, but afterwards he discovered it to be an emanation from the devil, or the devil himself. He prayed to the Virgin for guidance, and one night, looking on her image, he heard a great noise, like that of a cannon; the house shook, the windows of his chamber were smashed, and a rent was made in the wall of Loyola Castle which remains to this day. In the morning, fully recovered from his wound, Loyola started out for the monastery of Montserrat, a day's ride west of Barcelona.

35

VIRGIN BLACK

Montserrat, the Jagged Mountain, rises abruptly from the plain in one great mass of fantastic shapes, turrets, battlements and spires. The path to the monastery is cut zig-zag out of a cliff. Montserrat is the abode of the Black Madonna, which is said to have been sculpted from life by St Luke, the patron of art and medicine. Discovered in a cave by shepherds led by angels in the year 888, the statue had lain there since being brought to Spain by St Peter in the year 50. It represents the Virgin seated, with the infant Jesus in her lap. He is holding a pine cone, a symbol of the body of the god who dies and is restored again. Her extended hands hold two orbs. As to why she should be black, there are many competing theories. Centuries of candle smoke, for one; and some point to affinities with the dark goddesses Isis and Cybele, but we need not concern ourselves with these details here, for the Black Madonna has a real presence.

On 24 March 1522, the eve of the feast of the Annunciation, Ignatius of Loyola knelt down before this image. He had not eaten for days, save for a few wild herbs. The air was acrid with frankincense. Candles blazed and guttered at the icon's feet. As Loyola lifted his eyes to meet the Black Madonna's gaze, her mouth flickered in the candlelight. She spoke to him in a deep voice which reverberated through the church. As to what she said, Loyola tells us that she spoke in the language of Heaven, which cannot be translated into the dialects of mortals, but it concerned a great battle which would be fought for the salvation of the world.

In like manner, he once was granted an illumination of the Trinity, whose mystery he saw clearly with the eyes of the soul; but this vision was impossible to put into words. It sustained him throughout his life, as did the message of the Black Madonna. Immediately after receiving it, he stripped off his cavalier's outfit, hung up his sword and dagger, and put on a suit of sackcloth he had previously prepared. Thus he came to serve not the lady of his dreams, but the Empress of Heaven.

Ignatius of Loyola organized the Company of Jesus along military lines, with himself as Superior General. Before long, the Company possessed itself of all the strongholds which command the public mind – the pulpit, the press, the confessional, the academies. Wherever the Jesuit preached, the church was too small for the audience. The name of Jesuit on a title-page secured the circulation of a book. The Old World was not wide enough for this activity. The Company sent representatives to all the countries which the great maritime discoveries of the preceding age had laid open to European enterprise. They were to be found in the depths of the Peruvian mines, at the marts of the African slave-caravans, on the shores of the Spice Islands, in the observatories of China. In Japan, Francis Xavier presented the Mikado with a mechanical clock and musical box; in return, he was granted the use of an abandoned Buddhist monastery. The Jesuits also made converts in regions which neither avarice nor curiosity had tempted any of their countrymen to enter; and they preached and disputed in tongues which no other native of the West could understand.

You will be hearing more of our work in due course, said Fr Brown; but now, it is getting late, and it is time for bed.

36

BÉGUINE BLUE

That first night in Loyola House, my new companion Maeterlinck and I were shown to a long upstairs dormitory. An autumn moon shone through the tall uncurtained windows, throwing parallelograms of chill on to the bare boards. Already the other boys — some eighteen or twenty – seemed to be asleep, or feigning sleep. We were assigned adjoining beds. Our guide, a lay brother, watched as we undressed and got between the sheets. Then he bade us goodnight, and left.

When his footsteps had diminished into silence, Maeterlinck whispered to me, asking who I was and where I came from. I gave him a short resumé of my life thus far. Maeterlinck then told me this story:

As you might have guessed from my name, I am Flemish. I am given to understand that there are others of my nation in Loyola, for the relationship between Ireland and Flanders, as you know, extends for many centuries. I was born in Ghent. My parents died when I was young; my paternal uncle Maurice, a dealer in fine art, took me into his care. My earliest memories are of his rambling house at 6 Peperstraat — Rue du Poivre — whose very name recalls the spicy smells which breathed from every room, antique perfumes of brocades and calfskin bindings, the dusty aroma of old oil paintings. Ghent is a city of brooding, stagnant canals and winding alleyways, overlooked by tall gabled houses. Higher again rise the grim chateaux, the forbidding asylums, the chimneys of the cotton mills. There are bell towers everywhere, pervading the hours with their melancholy music.

Peperstraat leads on to the Grand Béguinage, whose inmates spend their lives in prayer and making lace. The Béguinage is in itself an image of Ghent, a labyrinth of streets, squares and chapels, surrounded by a gated wall and a moat. Often I would slip into this other world, wandering the cloisters or the herb gardens as the blue-robed sisters glided by in threes and fours, wearing headdresses that looked like swans. Come dusk, I would be lulled to sleep by their chanting at vespers, confusing it with the distant murmuring of bees.

My guardian, indeed, maintained an apiary at his summer house at Oostacker, some seven miles along the canal from Ghent to Terneuzen, not far from the Dutch frontier. Here, in the large garden that ran down to the water's edge, were twelve domes of straw, some of which he had painted a bright pink, some a clear yellow, but most of all a beguiling blue, for he had noticed the bees' fondness for this colour.

Come hither, my guardian would say, to the school of the bees,

and be taught the preoccupations of all-powerful nature, the inde-
fatigable organization of life, the lesson of ardent and
disinterested work; hear the music of these tuneful bearers of all
rural perfumes.

I spent many happy hours at Oostacker. The land was radiant
with little varnished houses, bright as new pottery, in which cup-
boards and clocks gleamed at the end of passageways. Barges
with sculptured poops and steamships bound for London or
Belfast sailed the elm-lined canal at the bottom of the garden. Yet
sometimes the sound of a fog-horn would penetrate my soul;
the countryside which once spread gladly out before me became
flat, monotonous, dreary; and my guardian's domain – the white
house with green shutters, the workshops, the conservatories,
the gardens, the beehives, the tower he had built in which to
study – seemed like a prison.

37

GILT

Until I was six, continued Maeterlinck, I was educated by a succession of Irish governesses, whom my uncle considered to speak better English than the English. With my uncle and his associates I spoke French; from the servants I learned Flemish. Thus, from an early age, I knew the danger of making categorical pronouncements; for there were at least three ways of saying things. At seven, I was sent to the school of the Benedictine nuns at the Nouveau Bois. Here I learned my prayers, the catechism, and some arithmetic. The schoolroom was hung with pictures of the saints and scenes from the Bible: Breughel's *Massacre of the Innocents*, in particular, made a deep impression on me, and I used to have nightmares in which I entered it, becoming one of its subjects.

After two years, I left for the Institut Central, a private school situated in the Rue du Paradis. After a sparse lunch of bread and jam, the pupils were allowed an hour of doing nothing; I used this interlude to explore my whereabouts. Close by was the great

Belfry of Ghent. The concierge of the tower was the watchmaker whose shop was situated at its base; as I got to know him, he would waive the one-franc entrance fee, and admit me to its dark, steep staircase. As I climbed, I would count the steps – one for every day of the year – before arriving at the summit. From here, the view embraced a greater part of Flanders, and an admirable survey of Ghent.

I would gaze down like a god, naming the constituents of my city: Place d'Armes, Rue de Congo, Parc de la Citadelle, Place du Casino, Hospice des Aliénés, Rue de la Paix, Hospice des Orphelins. When I ran out of given names, I would make up others; but the city was inexhaustible, and there were quarters which resisted all my powers of language. Sometimes, all of Ghent was shrouded in fog, while the weathervane on the belfry spire – a gilded dragon fifteen feet long – glittered in the sunlight. Then I imagined myself a pilot, or a sailor on the topmast. I would spend seeming hours aloft. Yet, miraculously, when I descended, the clocks in the watchmaker's shop would indicate that many minutes of freedom still remained.

From thence I would proceed to the Cathedral of St Bavon, a many-chambered space of nave, transepts, choirs, and chapels. Here was St Bavon himself, in his ducal robes, hovering among the clouds; Moses striking water from the rock, and the Raising of the Brazen Serpent; the Presentation in the Temple; the Queen of Sheba before Solomon; Christ among the Dukes of Burgundy; and many more. I would save the best to the last: the great altarpiece by the van Eyck brothers, Hubert and Jan. It is an immensely complex work, made in the shape of a folding screen:

when shut, the twelve outer panels show scenes relating to the Annunciation; opened, it becomes twice as big. These twelve inner panels centre on the Adoration of the Lamb. Ghent's patron saint, my uncle had pointed out to me, is John the Baptist; and the connection between his attribute, the Lamb of God, and the wool industry, which was the source of the city's once immense wealth, is clear.

Hundreds of figures are visible — angels, bishops, saints, pilgrims — clothed in rich brocades embroidered with precious stones and pearls. The central landscape is bejewelled with every kind of flower. The spires and towers of a perfect city glitter in the distance. In this scenery of Heaven, I could lose myself for an eternity, before returning, just on time, to the Institut Central.

38

PASSIONFLOWER

When I was eleven, my uncle happened to pick up a French grammar used by the pupils of the Institut, and noticed that the rules concerning the subjunctive and the past participle were inadequate. He himself had attended the Jesuit College of Namur, and this induced him to enter me as a boarder at the local Jesuit College, that of Sainte-Barbe. You know that St Barbara is invoked by architects and military engineers. Her patronage of this college is equally appropriate. In my fits of melancholy, as I have said, I used to think my uncle's country house at Oostacker was a prison; I did not know the meaning of the word until I entered the Collège de Sainte-Barbe.

The buildings of grey stone resembled a barracks; the windows were barred. The central courtyard, where the pupils took their exercise, was enclosed by high stone walls. Alone, on a gable, the implacable face of a big clock doled out the minutes and the hours. The chimes, mingling with those of the invisible, dead city beyond, fell on us like shadows. Everything was measured by the clock. At six, when the last stroke of the Angelus had trembled into silence, we would sit down to supper. As we began to eat, a priest would rise to the lectern and begin that evening's lesson.

Typically, these were meditations on the lives of the saints, or on fruit and flowers. Ghent, it was said, had invented the orangery: might the original paradisal fruit have been an orange? The passionflower, discovered by the Jesuits in the New World in the sixteenth century, had gained its name by its resemblance to the instruments of the Passion. The leaf was the spear; the tendrils, the whips; the ovary, the pillar; the corona, the crown of thorns; the stamens, the hammers; the three styles, the nails. Was the passionflower not living proof that God had preordained the Christian conquest of America?

As time went by, I became accustomed to these routines; but I found it difficult to reconcile myself to what passed for society in Sainte-Barbe. Friendship among boys was not encouraged. We were granted occasional weekend leave, and this I would pass with my uncle Maurice; but increasingly his business took him abroad. It was then determined that his brother, my uncle Franck, whom I scarcely knew at that stage, should look after me. Franck turned out to be a congenial fellow. Like me, he was an enthusiastic philatelist, and willingly indulged my weakness for the stamps of the Belgian Congo. He had, however, one peculiarity.

I was given to understand that some years ago he had been the victim of an unrequited passion. When he realized the hopelessness of his case, he purchased a parrot, whom he taught to pronounce the name of his lost love, Dympna. He also called the parrot Dympna. On my visits to his apartment in the Rue du Canard, he would talk to the parrot as if it were a human being, while it replied, Dympna, Dympna, to everything he said; he swore that his pet, by subtly altering the pitch and tone of its one-word vocabulary, could communicate a wide range of emotional and intellectual responses. I did not believe him, but after a while my ear became attuned to the modulations of its speech. From then on we enjoyed amicable three-way conversations.

One day I noticed that Dympna was looking rather listless. Her normally ebullient delivery had degenerated to a monotone. Franck was downcast. After some minutes, he went to his desk and took out a little pill-box, which he presented to me. It contains a special tea, he said, which I highly recommend. But only take it when absolutely necessary. And don't worry, you will know it when the time comes.

Shortly afterwards, I left the pair of them to an unaccustomed silence. Dympna did not even squawk goodbye. I never saw her or my uncle Franck again.

39

PARROT GREEN

A week went by, then two, then three. I was informed by the President General of the college that my uncle Franck had become incommunicado. After a month, my uncle Maurice came to see me. The President had set aside his own study for the visit, so I thought it must be a grave matter. What Maurice told me, briefly, was this:

Shortly after my last visit to Uncle Franck, Dympna had died. Franck had been inconsolable. He did not speak for a week, and then only to beg a neighbour for some hemp seed. At the time, the neighbour noticed a peculiar inflection in Franck's speech; only afterwards did he realize that it was a passable imitation of a parrot. From then on, it was believed, Franck thought he was the parrot. He began wearing fancy waistcoats. He would often repeat himself. On his few excursions to the outside world, he would strut rather than walk, and screech at passers-by. Such behaviour, though inappropriate, was harmless; and he was always well groomed.

Within a week or so, however, he was observed to perch on the stair-rail of the landing outside his apartment; and one day, he was found sprawled at the bottom of the stairwell. He was not seriously hurt, but my uncle Maurice, being sent for, decided that his increasing urge to fly would be best handled by professionals, who were commissioned to take him to the *maison de santé* in Gheel. On the journey there, he escaped during the night and was found the next morning perched in a tree. Persuading him to come down proved very difficult until one of his keepers had the idea of placing at the foot of the tree an enormous parrot-cage. On seeing this, he climbed down peaceably, was recaptured and taken to Gheel where, my guardian assured me, he was quite content.

That afternoon, I took the tea Uncle Franck had given me. At three o'clock, we were habitually served weak coffee to sustain us until supper time; I slipped the contents of the pill-box into my cup, drank it, and waited to see what would happen. For some time, nothing did. We returned to the schoolroom. It was 18 October, the feast of St Luke, patron of artists, and of the lace-makers of Ghent; and Fr Aloysius, our form master, had based his lesson on the first chapter of the Gospel according to Luke, which begins thus:

Forasmuch as many have taken in hand to set forth in order a declaration of those things which are most surely believed among us,

Even as they delivered them unto us, which from the beginning were eyewitnesses, and ministers of the word . . .

Luke, said Fr Aloysius, begins his account by directly connecting vision and speech, as if to say, those who see wonderful events must bear witness to them by their words. We further note that Luke alone among the four evangelists introduces the Angel Gabriel: an angel, a pure spirit, by definition incorporeal; yet he manifests himself to Mary in visible form, for it is written, *Mary saw him*. And he is sent by God to speak for Him. These indeed are great mysteries. Yet, as the Angel Gabriel announces, *With God nothing shall be impossible*; and Mary answers, *Be it unto me according to thy word*.

As Fr Aloysius proceeded with his exegesis, I saw again with my inward eye the Angel of the Annunciation as depicted in the St Bavon altarpiece. I saw the sculptured folds and crumples of his robes, his parted lips and his half-opened wings, whose upper edges are a bright parrot green.

40

FLANDERS BLUE

The morning, continued Maeterlinck, had been cold and hazy; as the day wore on, smoke from the factory chimneys lingered in the air until, by late afternoon, the world beyond the windows of the schoolroom had become opaque. Even within, sound was muffled, the master's voice a barely audible rumble. The pendulum of the wall-clock was poised at a motionless angle. I saw then that time had stopped. Fr Aloysius was arrested in mid-rhetorical gesture, the Gospel held in one hand, the other posed like a conductor's on the upbeat of a great symphony.

My gaze drifted to one of the gothic windows. The Angel Gabriel was framed, hovering against one of its trifoliate panes, his mouth pressed against the glass in an O of salutation. I rose from my desk, slowly at first, then more confidently as I got used to levitating. When I was eye-level with him, I glided towards him and emerged on the other side, leaving barely a ripple in the window-pane.

He took me in his arms and brought us almost to ground level;

then, hand in hand, we skimmed off over the cobbles. Even at this hour, the streets were thronged with men and women, looming from the oases of dulled light under lamp-posts with scarves wrapped around their mouths, hats pulled over their eyes. No one saw us come or go. Slowly, as we moved along, the fog began to dissolve; the Angel's body, too, began to disappear, as if his formal being had been bound by fog. The white robe shimmered, and was gone. Then the feet, the hands, the head. Only the smile and the wings remained, until they too melted into nothingness.

It was now bright sunlight, and I was alone in fifteenth-century Ghent. Gone were the dark-suited wraiths; instead, the street — it was Rue Longue de la Vigne, I realized — was flocked with bright colours, saffrons, bronze greens, Flanders blues. Ladies passed by in silk-hung litters with their armed consorts. Armour jingled, and the clack of wooden pattens resounded from the frosty pavement. The air swam with urgent perfumes: amber, musk, woodsmoke, horse-dung, the smell of dyed woollens and the starch of the ladies' headdresses, the nearby canal reeking of ammonia. Spices, too, were abundant, and a faint sharp scent of oranges. As the crowd brushed up against me, it did not take me under its notice.

When I arrived at the Square of St Bavon, a great ceremony was under way. Amidst a fanfare of trumpets, a griffin was lowered from the cathedral spire. As it beat its wings and opened its jaws, live birds flew out. Descending to the ground, it burst into flames, and a company of players emerged, one of whom bore the head of a man on a silver platter. A girl began to dance before it.

As I watched, I felt my body sway to her movements. Four of the company lit braziers, which exploded in clouds of incense. The girl spun faster and faster; I felt all the eyes of the crowd upon her, then the eyes of the crowd upon me. When I became the dancer, I lost consciousness. The next thing I knew, I was lying in the sick bay of the Collège de Sainte-Barbe, pinned beneath cold linen sheets.

There is little else to tell, said Maeterlinck. According to my classmates, I had fainted. I was diagnosed as suffering from nervous debilitation. My uncle Maurice came to see me within days, informing me that a change of climate would do me a world of good. Before long I was sent to Loyola House in the County of Down in Ireland, where you find me now.

That is my story.

41

CARBON BLACK

Over the next few weeks, Maeterlinck and I became friends. The Jesuits of Loyola House, like those of the College of St Barbara, did not approve of close relationships among boys. But the rule in Ireland, according to Maeterlinck, seemed comparatively relaxed, and in any case so labyrinthine were the premises that one could easily escape supervision.

It was difficult, indeed, to tell on which floor of Loyola House one happened to be at any given time: the corridors were full of unexpected landings, the staircases of twists and turnings. Rooms telescoped into other rooms. Alcoves led to annexes, and even a broom cupboard contrived to have a little window in it, through which one could look down into a high kitchen, where the lay brothers were preparing dinner or polishing the priests' boots.

Loyola House had formerly been Castlemourne, the seat of Lord Mourne, who decided, in 1776, to renovate the fifteenth-century fortress his family had inhabited for generations. He resolved on a neo-classical design, but Lady Mourne, an avid reader of the gothic novels then in vogue, was adamant that the new building should incorporate her taste. An accommodation was reached: the east half would be done in the classical mode, the west in the gothic. However, the interior frontier between these conflicting styles was not wholly resolved. Many rooms were disputed: some were left unfinished; some were fantastic compromises, in which gargoyles battled with representations of Greek gods. Meanwhile, the subterranean levels of cellars, vaults and magazines remained untouched.

Lord Mourne died in 1801, the year of the Act of Union of Great Britain and Ireland. He left no issue. Lady Mourne, despite many approaches, did not remarry, and died peacefully in 1829, the year of Catholic Emancipation. Only then was it revealed that she had secretly converted to Catholicism some years previously. She left Castlemourne to the Jesuits, but they, recognizing the political delicacy of the situation, did not take immediate possession. A nominally independent trust was established to develop the estate as a centre for the cultivation and study of rare species of plants; the existing orangery was considerably extended and provided with the most modern heating system then available. Rooms within the house were furnished as laboratories and herbariums. Much of the stock of Lord and Lady Mourne's library was relegated to an annex to accommodate a collection of botanical and associated theological literature.

Castlemourne was finally designated Loyola House on 31 July 1854, the feast day of St Ignatius of Loyola. Prospective pupils and their parents, drawn mostly from the Irish Catholic middle classes, attended in considerable numbers. After the inaugural

Mass, a portrait of St Ignatius, said to have been painted before his death, was solemnly installed in a special shrine, where it remains to this day. Its lifelike appearance, in which the eyes seem to follow the viewer, has often been remarked on; and the painted candle which illuminates Ignatius's features seems to burn with a real flame. He is shown holding an open book on which is inscribed the Jesuit motto, *Ad majorem Dei gloria*, though the words are scarcely legible, blackened as they are by centuries of actual candle smoke.

42

MOSS ROSE

It was a custom at Loyola on selected feast days for the Director-General to escort groups of boys on a guided tour of the orangery, in keeping with the Jesuit philosophy that the preconcerted design in the structure and fertilization of plants afforded a proof of the existence of God. Thus, on All Souls' Day, 1959, Maeterlinck and I found ourselves in a crocodile winding its way through a profusion of bamboos, tree ferns, palms, banana plants, cycads, orchids, overhanging mosses, and pitcher plants. The sub-tropical atmosphere dripped with outlandish perfumes; in the outside world beyond the curved glass walls it was freezing cold. As Fr Brown paused at a fork of the path, it began to snow.

The science of deduction and analysis is one which can only be acquired by long and patient study, nor is life long enough to allow any mortal to attain the highest perfection in it, said Fr Brown. Not my words, dear boys, but those of Sherlock Holmes. An unlikely source for a Jesuit priest to quote, you might think, but let us not forget that Arthur Conan Doyle, the creator of

Holmes, was himself educated at our great sister college, Stonyhurst in Lancashire. Indeed, during his years there, in the early 1870s, he formed a nodding acquaintance with our Jesuit poet, Fr Hopkins, who was near at hand in our seminary of St Mary's. I hope I am not stretching a point when I say that in Fr Hopkins's poetry we can see the signs of a budding detective, who could infer the existence of God from the beautiful appearance of a bluebell. For the whole universe is littered with His clues.

Furthermore, Arthur Conan Doyle was born on 22 May 1859, the feast day of St Rita of Cascia, the patron saint of desperate cases, to whom we resort when all other methods have failed: it is not difficult to see a parallel here with the great consulting detective. Let us also note Rita's association with the sense of smell. It is recorded that her meditations on the Passion of Christ were so intense that from 1441 until her death in 1457 she bore a suppurating wound in her forehead, as though pierced by a crown of thorns. And her feast day is marked by the blessing of roses; her body, preserved incorrupt in Cascia in a glass casket, exudes an odour of roses to this day.

How many times have we observed Holmes, like a blood-hound, sniff the air, as the after-scent of a murderer's tobacco pervades the room? Most famously, let us dwell on the moment in the case of the Naval Treaty, where Holmes, holding up the drooping stalk of a moss rose, falls into a reverie and speaks these words:

There is nothing in which deduction is so necessary as in religion. It can be built up as an exact science by the

reasoner. Our highest assurance of the goodness of
Providence seems to me to rest in the flowers. All other
things, our powers, our desires, our food, are really
necessary for our existence in the first instance. But this rose
is an extra. Its smell and its colour are an embellishment of
life, not a condition of it. It is only goodness which gives
extras, and so I say again that we have much to hope from
the flowers.

Here, Fr Brown paused again; we followed his gaze to where
the huge fronds of a palm tree brushed against the glass dome of
the roof, on which the snowflakes, falling, instantly dissolved.

43

HONEY

In *The Hound of the Baskervilles*, continued Fr Brown, Holmes states that there are seventy-five perfumes, which it is very necessary that a criminal expert should be able to distinguish from each other, and promptly recognize. That may be so, but the great apiarist von Frisch has shown that the legendary olfactory perceptions of the bee are, in fact, equivalent to those of a trained parfumier, who can discriminate between more than 700 scents. However, Dr Watson records elsewhere that Mr Holmes devoted his retirement to bee-keeping and produced a learned treatise on the subject, the *Practical Handbook of Bee Culture*, so perhaps his estimate of the number of perfumes was then revised upwards by these researches. We note in passing that the bee was adopted by Napoleon as his personal emblem; and when St Ambrose was a baby, bees settled on his lips, indicating that he would become famous for his honeyed words.

But we need not delve further into the deep symbolism of the bee. For the moment, let us merely breathe the perfume of the blooms around us. Of all the senses, that of smell is the most intangible and yet the most deep-rooted, the most quick to waken long-dormant memories. When I smell turf smoke, I am immediately brought back to my childhood holidays in Donegal. I hear again the wild Atlantic roar; again I see the dazzling white-washed houses, under a rain-washed blue sky; I taste the salt on my lips. An aroma can induce visions. The poet Camoëns, singing of the glories of Vasco da Gama, evokes his explorations through the medium of scent: Socotra, famous for its bitter aloes; Sumatra, home of the strange tree which weeps tears of ben-zoin, more fragrant than all the myrrh of Arabia; the Isles of Banda, gay with the multicoloured nutmeg flower; Tidor and Tinaté, pungent with the smell of cloves; Tisian-Pa, where grows the aromatic sandalwood.

And in the wake of those early voyagers, led by the promise of cargo-loads of spice, our pioneering Jesuit fathers followed. We stand, dear boys, in a microcosm of that once brave new world. In this conservatory are reproduced the fruits and flowers which they harvested, together with countless souls. Breathe in this atmosphere, and you breathe the history of the Church, which constantly regenerates itself, as laid down in the Book of Genesis: *And God said, Behold, I have given you every herb bearing seed, which is upon the face of the earth, and every tree, in which is the fruit of a tree yielding seed; to you it shall be for meat.* That is, sustenance not only for the body, but food for thought, and for the soul. Such is the seed of faith, which has been implanted in you all. *The kingdom of heaven is like to a grain of mustard seed, which a man took, and sowed in his field: Which is indeed the least of all seeds: but when it is grown, it*

is the greatest among herbs, and becometh a tree, so that the birds of the
air come and lodge in the branches thereof . . .

Mesmerized by Fr Brown's words, I found myself gazing again at the lofty branches of the palm tree. Beyond the glass roof, it had stopped snowing; the sky was a heavenly blue, and one could think it the height of summer. I thought of flying, free as a bird.

The two boys at the back, said Fr Brown, are not paying attention. They appear to be thinking of higher things.

I looked towards him; he was pointing at Maeterlinck and me. I began to protest that I was indeed wrapped in his words.

Enough! said Fr Brown. You will see me in my study after evening chapel. Hereby endeth the lesson.

44

ULTRA-VIOLET

After dinner, Maeterlinck and I compared notes. When I asked him what had been passing through his mind when interrupted by the Director-General, he said he had been dreaming that he was in his uncle Maurice's summer home at Oostacker. Outside the window of the bedroom where he lay he could hear the murmuring of bees going about their business, and he pictured the glass hive in his uncle's study.

The seething comb of black and amber bodies seemed without purpose, but he knew that this was far from the case: by dancing, by touch, by scent, by the vibrations of their wings, bees communicated a map of the immediate nectar-bearing countryside. Maeterlinck imagined seeing the world through the multi-faceted eye of the bee – a grainy world, like needlepoint, composed of dots of information, in which no red is visible but lit with ultra-violet beyond the range of human sight. Moreover, the bee's visual system has a high flicker-fusion frequency, so that if a bee were to watch a motion picture, it would see isolated frames connected by moments of darkness, and would not be deluded into thinking that the images moved.

Of course, said Maeterlinck, as to what the bee really perceives, we can have no idea; but then, can we know at all the inner experience of our fellows when they call the colours with the same names as we do ourselves? No man's eye has ever looked into the mind of another.

The scent of plum-blossom drifted in through the window, and a fog-horn sounded from the Terneuzen canal, drowning the noise of the bees for a moment. He looked out: at the bottom of the garden, a steam-packet was gliding by, its rails lined with passengers; gulls flocked in its wake. He wished he had wings to fly off into the world beyond, when he was summoned back to reality by the voice of Fr Brown.

I was elated when he told me his dream. It occurred to me then that Maeterlinck could be the brother I had never had. I told him that, when staring up at the glass roof of the conservatory, I had noticed how its cast iron frame resembled the ribs of the palm leaves which brushed against it, and I thought then of the structure as a living organism, blown from the breath of a god and still trembling in the winter sunshine. My soul had burst the glassy bubble and soared up into the outside. The air was razor-sharp. I could smell snow and the skeins of turf smoke that rose from the whitewashed farmhouses dotted across the countryside. From this bird's eye view I could see the whole of Loyola House and realized its extent was even greater than I had suspected: a great castellated mass, with many different pitches of roofs and dormer windows overlooking courtyards, stables, barns, greenhouses, all located in a further maze of walled gardens and interconnecting avenues. Down on the coast road a black Morris Oxford was puttering along, emitting little white puffs from its exhaust pipe, like bursts of code, and I thought for a second it might be my uncle Celestine coming to see me; but it turned off into a farm laneway and disappeared. Still, I was consoled by the letter I had got that morning from my cousin Berenice. I had been about to read it over in my mind when the Director-General's voice broke in, calling me back to the base world.

Would you like to read the letter? I asked. Maeterlinck replied that he would be most privileged.

45

BEESWAX

Dear coz,

I hope this letter finds you well. I am sorry it took me so long to reply to yours, but they keep us very busy at St Dympna's, in fact the Mother Superior says she wants her girls to be as busy as bees, and it is a regular hive of industry. They are teaching us to write in paragraphs, as you will notice from this letter. It says in the book that a paragraph is a distinct division of written or printed matter that begins on a new, usually indented line, consists of one or more sentences, and typically deals with a single thought or topic or quotes one speaker's continuous words. So whether we speak in paragraphs or not is anybody's guess.

Another thing, they say it is good style not to repeat the same word on any given page, but of course this is nonsense, because otherwise you would hardly be able to write 'a' or 'the' or 'and'. I see I have already used the word 'letter' twice in the same paragraph, so there you are. And the word 'paragraph', for that matter.

Anyway, you remember I told you that the Mother Superior has a copy of the Picture in her office. Well, the other day we were all queueing for communion, and you know the way there's a bank of candles in front of our Lady's shrine, well, I picked off some of the wax drippings, because I love squidging it up and rolling it between my fingers and thumb, and Mother Superior spotted me and I had to go and see her in her office afterwards.

So she starts telling me how, unlike the chapels in ordinary schools, the candles in St Dympna's are all real beeswax, and if I only knew how hard the bee has to work just to make a little flake of wax I wouldn't be so profligate with it. Then she goes on about the virginity of bees and how the wax is a symbol of the Blessed Virgin, and the wick is the soul of Christ, and the flame is the Holy Ghost, and she points to the Picture. You remember the candle in the Picture, well, I swear it looked as if it was really burning. For a minute I thought I was going to faint but I pulled myself together.

In fact, fainting is quite popular at St Dympna's, which is hardly any wonder when you consider the lumpy porridge and the mutton pie, and some of the girls do it all the time to get out of class. But they found one of the girls fainted outside the dormitory the other night, and everybody is saying she must have seen the ghost nun I told you about, that haunts the corridor, and some of the other girls swore

they heard her rattling her chains. Personally I heard
nothing, but they packed this girl who had fainted off to
Belgium, because when they finally brought her around she
was paralysed for a week, and they have doctors in Belgium
to look after that kind of thing.

The Mother Superior gave me an imposition, which was
to write out this poem ten times in my best handwriting –

> *Th' industrious bee extracts from every flower*
> *Its fragrant sweets, and mild balsamic power;*
> *Learn thence, with greatest care and nicest skill*
> *To take the good, and to reject the ill:*
>
> *By her example taught, enrich thy mind;*
> *Improve kind nature's gifts, by sense refined;*
> *Be thou the honeycomb, in whom may dwell*
> *Each mental sweet, nor leave one vacant cell.*

So you can see the old M.S. has bees on the brain. If you
ask me, this place is getting curiouser and curiouser. What
about you?

Fondest regards –

Berenice.

46

CAMEL

This is most interesting, said Maeterlinck. That your cousin should have encountered a philosophy of bees a day or two before similar thoughts had occurred to me is not in itself unusual; but given the extra dimension of the painting by van Eyck, whose work seems to have influenced my life, and yours, and hers, it would seem that we three are fated to be a part of a story whose purpose is as yet inscrutable.

Indeed, it puts me in mind of a story told to me by my uncle Maurice. It concerns the origin of the word 'serendipity'. One day he happened to send me on an errand to buy some turpentine, for which he gave me a one-franc piece. Alas! When I reached the artists' supplier and put my hand into my pocket, the money was missing. But when I retraced my steps, searching the pavement and the gutter for the lost coin, I found instead a five-franc note wedged in the bars of a storm-grating. When I related this to my uncle, he told me it was an instance of serendipity, an English word which had long intrigued him.

After some research, he discovered that it had been coined by Horace Walpole, the author of the gothic novel, *The Castle of Otranto*. Walpole applied this notion of serendipity to curious or happy chains of events, on the model of a tale called *The Three Princes of Serendip*, in which the said princes, as they travelled, were always making discoveries, by accident or sagacity, of things they were not in quest of: for instance, one of them discovered that a camel blind in the right eye had travelled the same road lately, because the grass was eaten only on the left side.

When my uncle tried to locate this book in the Ghent Public Library, he was told it did not exist; upon further enquiry, he was given to understand that Walpole, it was surmised, had read it under the name *Voyage des trois princes de Serendip*, a French translation of an Italian translation made by an Armenian of an alleged Persian original. Alas! When he asked if he could consult this volume, the librarian told him that it was missing from its shelf, and had been for some time, since identical requests had been made over the years. One of the most curious, indeed, was by a brain surgeon who phoned the library in the middle of a delicate operation, thinking that the book might inspire him on how to proceed.

But in any event, there existed another version of the *Voyage*, by Voltaire, who had taken its broad outlines to create his romance, *Zadig*. The librarian was delighted to obtain this book for my uncle. My uncle hurried out of the library with his prize under his arm. So overjoyed was he at locating at least one source of the mysterious word that he decided to celebrate by repairing to a nearby public house, where he ordered a large measure of hot gin. He drank the gin, went home and opened the book in a pleasant haze of expectation. Alas! What he now held in his hands was not *Zadig*, but something entirely different, *Le crayon bleu*, by an author whose name was totally unfamiliar to him.

He remembered then that he had shared a booth in the public house with a studious-looking man. A blue book had been on the table. *Zadig* was a blue book. He had lifted the wrong one. Happily, when he dashed back to the venue, he found the man engrossed in the library's precious copy of *Zadig*.

Do sit down, said the studious man. I am reading a most interesting story. Shall I give you its gist?

47

GOLD

During the reign of King Moabdar in Babylon there lived a young man named Zadig. He married, but he found that the first moon of marriage, as written in the book of Zend, is of honey, and the second of wormwood. After a time he got rid of his wife and retired to a house in the country on the banks of the Euphrates, where he sought to find happiness in the study of nature. He soon became so versed in the ways of animals and plants that he could see a thousand differences where other men see uniformity.

One day he was out walking when he met one of the queen's eunuchs, in a great hurry, followed by several officers looking about them in visible distress.

Young man, cried the Chief Eunuch, you haven't by any chance seen the queen's dog?

It's not a dog, said Zadig, it's a bitch.

So it is, said the Chief Eunuch.

It's a small spaniel, added Zadig, and she's just pupped; she's lame in the left forefoot and she has very long ears.

You've seen her, then? said the Chief Eunuch.

Not a bit of it, answered Zadig, I never even knew the queen had a bitch.

Meanwhile, just at that moment, back at the palace, by one of the usual freaks of fortune, the king's best horse bolted from the stable and fled into the plains of Babylon, pursued by the Master of the King's Hounds and his underlings. They met up with Zadig.

Have you seen the king's horse pass by? cried the Master of the Hounds.

The horse you're looking for is the best galloper in the stable, said Zadig. It's fifteen hands high, with a small hoof, and a tail three and a half feet long. The studs on its bit are twenty-three carat gold, and its shoes eleven scruple silver.

Which road did it take? cried the Master of the Hounds.

Damned if I know, said Zadig, I never heard tell of it till just now.

Zadig was then hauled before the Chief Justice and condemned to be flogged and spend the rest of his days in the salt mines of Siberia, for the Master of the Hounds and the Chief Eunuch were convinced he had stolen the horse and the bitch. But lo and behold, no sooner was judgement passed than the horse and the bitch were found. Reluctantly, the judges withdrew their sentence, but fined Zadig four hundred ounces of gold for having denied seeing what he had seen. Only after the fine was paid was he allowed to plead his case, which he did in the following manner:

Stars of Justice, he said, Unfathomable Wells of Knowledge,

Mirrors of Truth, that have the weightiness of lead, the hardness of iron, the radiance of the diamond, and much affinity with gold, since I am permitted to speak before this august assembly, I swear by all the gods that I have never seen the queen's honourable bitch or the king of king's sacred horse. Allow me to explain.

48

PENCIL BLUE

I was walking towards the little wood where I later met the venerable Chief Eunuch and the most illustrious Master of the Hounds, said Zadig. I saw an animal's tracks in the sand; it was not hard to judge that they were those of a small dog. Between the tracks of the paws were long, shallow furrows: these had to be the marks of a bitch with dangling teats, who therefore had had pups recently. Beside the tracks of the forepaws were other marks, which suggested she had long ears. The sand was less hollowed by one paw than by the three others. I concluded that she must be lame.

As for the king's horse, I saw on the road hoofprints all equal distances apart: this horse was a perfect galloper. The road was seven feet wide, and dust had been raised on the trees on either side. The horse had galloped down the middle, sweeping up the dust with his tail, which had to be three and a half feet long. I observed that the lower canopy of the trees came to five feet above the ground. Some leaves had been knocked down where the horse's head had brushed against them: he was therefore about fifteen hands high. As regards the bit, it had to be of twenty-three carat gold because there were traces of that element on a stone I knew to be a touchstone, for I had tested it on another occasion. The shoes? I examined the pebbles on the road: some of them bore marks which could only have been made by eleven scruple silver.

The judges were most impressed by Zadig's logic. Before long the whole palace had heard of his deductions, and though some of the Magi thought he should be burned as a witch, the king ordered the fine of four hundred ounces of gold to be returned to him. The clerk of the court, the ushers, the attorneys, all called on him with great pomp to bring him his money, of which they only kept back three hundred and ninety-eight ounces towards legal costs.

Zadig saw how dangerous it was sometimes to appear to know too much, and promised himself that in future whatever he saw, he would say nothing.

Such an occasion soon presented itself. A state prisoner escaped and passed beneath the window of Zadig's house. When questioned, he made no reply, but it was proved beyond doubt that he had looked out of the window. For this crime he was fined five hundred ounces of gold. As was the custom in Babylon, he thanked the judges for their indulgence.

When he got home, he cried to himself, Ye gods! Pity the man who walks in a wood where the queen's bitch or the king's horse have passed! How dangerous it is to look out of the window! How difficult it is to be happy in this life!

*

My uncle, said Maeterlinck, thanked the studious man for his account of the Zadig story by buying him a drink, whereupon they proceeded to discuss the pleasure to be had from books.

But what, enquired my uncle, was the subject of *Le crayon bleu*, which he had mistakenly brought home?

It is a murder mystery, replied the studious man, in which the victim, a censor of literature, is found stabbed in the left eye by his own blue pencil, which has penetrated to the brain. How the detective arrives at the solution is most ingenious. May I give you the gist of the plot?

Perhaps, said Maeterlinck, I will tell you the studious man's version of *Le crayon bleu* on another occasion; but for now, I believe we have an appointment with Fr Brown.

49

JAFFA ORANGE

Maeterlinck knocked on the door of Fr Brown's study. A voice bade us enter. Fr Brown was seated in an armchair beside a cheerful coal fire.

Do sit down, and make yourselves comfortable, he said, and help yourselves to the tea and Jaffa Cakes. An excellent product, if I might venture, in which we experience a trinity of gustative experiences, as the sweet viscous orange centre is sandwiched between the hard dark bitter chocolate upper layer and the sponge biscuit base. Its name always recalls to me the Jaffa Gate of Jerusalem, by which one enters that city when visiting the Church of the Holy Sepulchre. Remind me to describe its splendours to you on another occasion.

But for now, we have other things to talk about. Let me begin by saying that I have not summoned you here in order to reproach you for your apparent distraction during my lesson this morning. Quite the opposite. I have been a priest and a teacher for many years and, by the grace of God, I have learned to identify promise in a boy by the look in his eyes, which are the windows of the soul. When I observed you looking up at the beautiful tracery of glass and cast iron which is one of the glories of Loyola House, I knew that you both possessed the faculty of visualization to a high degree. You will be familiar by now with the fine portrait of St Ignatius in the chapel, and you will have remarked how his eyes seem to glow with an inner light, because to him, his daydreams were vivid realities. It was just such a look I saw in you two.

In this you also resemble the French, for there are many in that nation who can perceive all the rooms of an imaginary house by a single mental glance, the walls and floors being made as if of glass; and others who have the habit of recalling scenes, not from the point of view whence they were observed, but from a distance, and they visualize their selves as actors on a mental stage. The peculiar ability the French show in prearranging ceremonials and *fêtes* of all kinds, and their undoubted genius for tactics and strategy, show that they are able to foresee effects with unusual clearness. Their phrase, '*figurez-vous*', or 'picture to yourself', seems to express their dominant mode of expression; our equivalent of 'imagine' is ambiguous.

We need boys with imagination. Boys who can, by intense concentration, lift themselves beyond the merely superficial and mundane. *That thine eyes may be open towards this house night and day*, as the author of the Book of Kings put it. Matthew records our Lord as saying, *The light of the body is the eye; if therefore thine eye be single, thy whole body shall be full of light*. Single: that is, single-minded. And again, *While ye have light, believe in the light*.

I gather that you are both familiar with the work of the Flemish master Jan van Eyck. You, Maeterlinck, in particular, for you have been privileged to set eyes on his great altarpiece in Ghent. You will have observed how the central image of the *Adoration of the Lamb* is flooded with heavenly light, in which everything glitters, from the towers of the new Jerusalem on the horizon to the profusion of meticulously depicted flowers in the foreground. So convincing is this imaginative reality that van Eyck must have seen it with his inward eye. He painted what he saw, everything embodied in the medium of light, for the greater glory of God: *ad majorem Dei gloria*.

But let me return to van Eyck on another occasion. For now, I want to relate to you my recollections of another deeply religious man, the philosopher Ludwig Wittgenstein, whose acquaintance I made some years ago, when he worked as a gardener here, in Loyola House.

50

WITTGENSTEIN BLUE

I first got to know Wittgenstein, said Fr Brown, when I was out one day walking and reading my breviary in one of the herb gardens. At the time he was living in one of the potting sheds: such asceticism, I discovered later, was quite in character. As I passed by this mean abode, I heard him call out some remark or other about the weather. I stopped and greeted him, and, looking in through the door of the shed, noticed that he was lying on a sack of gravel, holding a copy of an American detective magazine, *Black Mask*. I hasten to say that I was not an aficionado of this rather hard-boiled publication, being more devoted, as you might have guessed, to the more cerebral pleasures of the Conan Doyle school of writing. Nevertheless, it afforded some pretext for conversation.

You enjoy murder mysteries? I asked.

Mysteries, yes, replied Wittgenstein.

And murder?

Murder is a device whereby the detective can exercise his

ethical power, and restore a moral universe. However, the detective in the *Black Mask* stories is not a thinking being; he is a man of action, who knows the uselessness of words. This I enjoy.

But surely there must be a point where the detective is called upon to explain his actions?

Ah. I see you have not read many *Black Mask* stories, said Wittgenstein. But there are admittedly instances in which the protagonist, finding himself in a lull of the action, sometimes muses about his surroundings. Usually, this is merely atmospheric; but such details make philosophy, since the world, especially in detective stories, is everything that is the case. Hence, in the story I have just been reading, the detective is alone on the deck of a ship in the middle of the night, with no sound but the ticking of the ship's clock. A clock, says the detective, is a bewildering instrument at best: measuring a fragment of infinity: measuring something which does not perhaps exist.

I was greatly taken by this thought, said Wittgenstein, for it almost precisely mirrors a thought of St Augustine's, as expressed in his *Confessions*: *I am not measuring the future, because it does not yet exist; nor the present, because it has no extent; nor the past, because it no longer exists*.

You are familiar with the *Confessions*? I asked, somewhat naively.

Wittgenstein's singularly blue eyes blazed at me from the darkness of the potting shed.

It is the most serious book in the world, he whispered.

He then proceeded to quote me whole paragraphs of the *Confessions* in St Augustine's beautiful Latin.

Thereafter I made a point of visiting Wittgenstein during my free periods, for I saw that we had much in common. Sometimes I would find him weeding, or transplanting herbs, in which cases he would sometimes ruminate about their properties, of which he possessed an encyclopaedic knowledge. At other times he would discourse about seemingly unrelated matters. For instance, he had spent some time in Dublin, where he used to frequent Bewley's Oriental Café in Grafton Street.

An excellent place, he would say, there must be very good management behind this organization; and he would then extol the perspicacity of its staff, who knew exactly what he wanted to eat each day — a plain omelette and a coffee — without his having to ask. This would then lead him into speculating on the virtues of silence.

One day he greeted me abruptly with these words: Before Christ, people experienced God — or Gods — as something outside themselves. But since Christ, people — not all, but those who have learnt to see through him — see God as something in themselves.

Since this is the case, said Fr Brown, let me attempt to give you a short biography of Wittgenstein, for knowledge of men's lives enables us more clearly to see God's purpose, as exemplified by the *Lives of the Saints*.

51

RHINOCEROS BLACK

Ludwig Wittgenstein was born at 8.30 p.m. on 26 April 1889, the eighth and youngest child of Karl Wittgenstein, who had made an immense fortune as the creator of Austria's pre-war iron and steel industry. As a child Ludwig was not especially brilliant – his brothers appeared much more gifted – but at the age of eight he paused in a doorway to consider the question, Why should one tell the truth if it is to one's advantage to tell a lie?

Finding no satisfactory answer, he concluded that there was, after all, nothing wrong with lying under such circumstances. He passed on through the doorway and sat down to dinner with the family. Nevertheless, that question, or similar questions, were to remain with him for the rest of his life.

Call me a truth-seeker, he once wrote to his sister, and I will be satisfied.

He appeared not especially brilliant: yet he had an extraordinary aural and visual imagination. From an early age he could whistle with great accuracy and expression, and during his philosophical career in Cambridge, he and his associate David Pinsent developed a method of performing Schubert songs, Pinsent playing the piano, and Wittgenstein whistling. At the age of ten, he constructed a sewing-machine from empty cotton reels, dowelling rods, elastic bands and bits of wire, which actually sewed a few stitches: he had, he said, merely visualized the components of a real machine, and then reproduced them.

This mechanical aptitude led him to become a student of aeronautical engineering, then in its infancy. In the summer of 1908 he emigrated to England, where he performed important experiments at the Kite Flying Upper Atmosphere Station near Glossop in Derbyshire. He also made several successful balloon ascents, which were to stand him in good stead in later life, for he once told me that doing philosophy was like making a map of an unknown terrain. Floating high above the landscape, he saw that there were many different routes to any destination; the difficulty lay in reconciling such a view to the practicalities of the earthbound traveller.

In the autumn of that year, he proceeded to Manchester University, where he drew up plans for a jet reaction propeller for aircraft, a proposal so far ahead of the available technology that he was viewed by some of his colleagues as a lunatic. Despairing of being understood, he turned to pure physics, and thence to the philosophy of mathematics, in whose austere realms he found some consolation. Yet the business of truth and lies still concerned him. Mathematics offered a view of the universe in which lies were a logical impossibility. There could be no decisions to make there, for the eternal truth of number lay beyond such moral considerations. Only in language could free will be exercised. *By thy word thou shalt be justified*, says Mark's Gospel.

This quandary led him to Bertrand Russell, then regarded as the foremost British philosopher. On 18 October 1911 (the feast day of St Luke, patron saint of artists), he burst unannounced into Russell's rooms in Cambridge, saying that he had developed a passion for philosophy, which he wished to pursue further with him. Wittgenstein proceeded to visit Russell almost daily. Russell found him argumentative and tiresome. When, on All Souls' Day, 2 November, Russell asked him to admit that there was not a rhinoceros in the room, Wittgenstein would not.

I have considered this proposition many times, said Fr Brown, and my interpretation of Wittgenstein's refusal to admit the absence of a rhinoceros in the room goes as follows:

52

UNICORN WHITE

When Marco Polo travelled to the Far East, all medieval tradition had convinced Europeans of the existence of the unicorn, an animal that looked like a gentle and slender white horse with a long horn on its muzzle. But since it proved increasingly difficult to find unicorns in Europe, it was decided that the creatures were only to be found in exotic countries, such as the kingdom of Prester John in Ethiopia.

Marco Polo was thus looking for unicorns. On his return from China, he visited Java, where he saw some animals which he identified as unicorns. Admittedly, they were not white, but black. Their hides resembled those of buffaloes, their hooves those of elephants. Their horns were much shorter than what one would expect. They were not particularly gentle, and they were far from being slender. What Marco Polo saw was the rhinoceros. Nevertheless, it was a unicorn, for all his reading of medieval romances had led him to identify it as a unicorn.

Wittgenstein, as I have remarked, had an acute visual imagination. It would have been no problem for him to see a
rhinoceros – or a unicorn, for that matter – in his mind's eye; or,
indeed, under Russell's table. When Russell, as he reports himself, made a great play of looking under tables and chairs in an
effort to convince Wittgenstein that there was no rhinoceros
present, this was a failure of Russell's imagination. It was also a
refusal to acknowledge that a verbal rhinoceros has as much presence as a verbal unicorn. For both can be imagined, and
described through language, which has the power of creating
worlds beyond that of empirical observation.

It was appropriate, then, that Wittgenstein's chief recreation,
besides reading detective stories, was going to the cinema, where
he could absorb himself in the moving pictures of a purely imaginary world. He was especially fond of musicals and westerns; he
abhorred newsreels and anything of a documentary nature. Not
long after our first meeting, he asked if I would drive him to
Newcastle to see a 'flick'. I confess that my education had led me
to consider such entertainments as essentially frivolous, but such
was the force of Wittgenstein's personality that I readily agreed.
That Saturday, on his afternoon off, I drove him to the Arcadia
cinema in Newcastle. By pure coincidence, it was 3 April, the
feast day of St Richard de Wyse of Chichester, the patron saint of
coachmen.

On the way to Newcastle, Wittgenstein engaged me in a conversation about William James's *Varieties of Religious Experience*, a
book which had deeply impressed him when he had first read it in
1911. This then led him to discuss James's *Principles of Psychology*,

which he disliked for its pragmatic method; nevertheless, it contained an anecdote which he found most interesting, for it raised some profound questions about the nature of personality. I confessed I was unfamiliar with the work of William James, though I had once, in my teens, read a novella by his brother Henry, *The Turn of the Screw*, which had disturbed my sleep for some weeks.

Wittgenstein was about to relate the anecdote in question when he saw that we had arrived at the Arcadia. A wild light appeared in his eyes; he broke off his narrative abruptly, promising to return to it at a more appropriate juncture.

I was pleasantly surprised to see that the main feature was called *Only Angels Have Wings*.

53

PANEL-LAMP RED

We made our way into the cinema. Wittgenstein insisted on paying the admission price; later I was to discover that his generosity was such that, on inheriting a vast fortune after his father's death, he signed it all away to other members of his family. We were shown down through the darkened auditorium by a pillbox-hatted usherette bearing a torch. Wittgenstein insisted on sitting in the front row. The opening feature was a newsreel. It was 1951, and images were shown of the IRA campaign at that time: a mangled electricity pylon, a broken dam, a derailed train. Wittgenstein wriggled in his seat impatiently, clenching his fists and hissing, This is not the real thing.

When the main feature appeared, I realized my expectations were to be confounded: I had, you might say, mistaken a rhinoceros for a unicorn, for the angels of the title were purely metaphorical. The story concerned a company of air pilots in South America, led by the actor Cary Grant. Their mission was to ferry mail from one isolated station to the other, over the high *cordillera* of the Andes. In this they accorded with the Greek *angelos*, a messenger. Once I realized this, I settled down quite comfortably. The film looked most atmospheric, and I began to see that a world composed in black and white can hint at colours otherwise unnameable, the subtle colours of the soul.

There is a girl. Nevertheless the aeronauts continue their business, communicating through rickety black radio telephones. One of them looks out for weather from a mountain outpost, and signals the approaching storms. An expected aeroplane is listened for in vain, till it buzzes suddenly out of the darkness and swoops across the waving palm trees. These actions are repeated over and over in various combinations. Either the plane will land safely, or it will not. The pilots all smoke, and this becomes a rhythm of their talk, or the talk itself.

A new pilot appears on the scene. He wears a suit and a tie and a Homburg hat. He smokes. He is not all he seems. Once upon a time, we hear, he parachuted from a stricken plane and left his radio operator behind to die. The new pilot has brought along his wife, who, before the time of the film, had been going with Cary Grant.

This is the gist of the circumstances. As to what happens, I will not reveal the outcome, for I would not like to spoil it for you, should you decide to see it some day. But it contains sequences of great beauty, and I can still visualize the dim red panel-lamps in the cockpit, and the dials with their radium-tinted numbers emitting a pale star-like glow. Then to rise clear above the cloud-bank: such sudden brightness, you never thought the clouds at night could dazzle. It is like flying through some strange limbo.

Everything now grows luminous – the pilot's hands, his flying gear, his wings. For the light does not stream from the stars: it wells up from underneath in endless white drifts. He floats through a milky stream of light. When he looks around, he sees the radio operator smiling.

Out of the corner of my eye I saw Wittgenstein, with great excitement, visibly absorb himself in the screen, as if he were one of the actors, as if it were his hands on the joystick, his mouth holding the cigarette, his eyes reflecting the stars. I had never seen a man so animated: watching him, you might be watching the film itself.

When the film came to the end, Wittgenstein slumped down in his seat like one exhausted.

54

DANUBE BLUE

We emerged from the dark cave of the picture-house, rubbing our eyes. It was broad daylight: the edges of things trembled and shimmered. An ozone-laden breeze gusted in from the sea-front. I felt quite light-headed, and suggested to Wittgenstein that we have some tea. We entered a nearby café, where he ordered a pot of tea, and a glass of water for himself. When we were settled, he began to talk animatedly, all the while manipulating the salt and pepper cellars as illustration to his narrative.

You remember the scene in the flick, he said, when the pilot and his radio operator find themselves above the storm. They wander through a dense treasure hoard of stars, where absolutely nothing is alive but them. They are like those robbers of fabled cities, immured within the sparkling chambers from which there is no escape. Amid the frozen gems they wander, infinitely rich yet doomed.

They are victims of *Sehnsucht*, that Germanic yearning for a world beyond the world. I think of the ghostly whisper heard by the protagonist of Schubert's song, 'The Wanderer': *There, where you are not, only there is happiness*. For we make the stars return our gaze; we give the constellations names, that they might resemble us. We see Heavenly Twins everywhere. So it is in the Schubert song, '*Die Sternennächte*', 'Starry Nights', composed by him on an October night in 1819, as the stars blazed at the window of his cramped garret in Vienna.

Wittgenstein was silent for a moment. Then, taking the salt cellar, he began to move it on the tablecloth around the sugar bowl, all the while whistling a little eerie tune. When it had drawn to its close, he lifted his eyes towards mine, and spoke:

> *On moonlit nights, my broken heart*
> *Finds peace among the stars;*
> *Yet this flawed world of ours is decked*
> *With galaxies of flowers.*
>
> *Perhaps the stars feel heartbreak too,*
> *As they shine serenely on:*
> *Perhaps, for them, our earth's a star*
> *That shines at break of dawn.*

Forgive my translation. The original is by Johann Baptist Mayrhofer, who shared that long dark room in the Wipplingerstrasse with Schubert for two years. Poor Mayrhofer! A tortured, woman-hating man, who had spent ten years with the monks at the monastery of St Florian until, feeling himself unworthy, he had turned to law, and thence to poetry. St Florian, as you will know, is the patron of Austria, but also of brewers. So Mayrhofer found himself torn between vocations, swaying between bouts of melancholia and gruff hilarity. Yet the marriage of his words and Schubert's music seems made in heaven. Perhaps those two years were the happiest of Mayrhofer's life, as poet and composer circled each other, not knowing which was the celestial body, which the satellite, as they were rapt in each other's orbits. Schubert died at the age of thirty on 19 November 1828. Eight years later, Mayrhofer ended his life in the Danube.

What do we know of ourselves? I, too, have done my time with the monks. I have cut myself off from the world, only to find myself return to it. I have climbed the glaciers of Iceland, and have stared into Norwegian fjords. I have inhabited the wilds of Connemara. I am of no fixed abode. I speak to you in a language which is not mine. Yet I need someone to speak to.

Sometimes I think that, for all I know, I might be someone else. In the anecdote I was about to relate to you before we entered the Arcadia, that is precisely what happens to its subject: unknown to himself, he becomes someone else. It is a condition known as fugue.

55

BOURNE BROWN

Ansel Bourne (said Wittgenstein) was born in 1826. The son of divorced parents, he had spent an unhappy childhood and had later become an itinerant carpenter in small Rhode Island towns. He was an atheist and, at 3 o'clock on 28 October 1857, he publicly declared that he would rather be deaf and mute than attend church. Moments later, he lost his hearing, speech and sight. On 11 November, he went to the church with a written message announcing his conversion. At noon on the following Sunday, 15 November, he rose up in the church and proclaimed that God had cured him of his infirmities. This alleged miracle brought him great prestige, and henceforth Bourne combined his carpenter trade with that of preacher. Some years later, he lost his wife. His second marriage was unhappy.

Thirty years went by in this fashion, with Bourne travelling from small town to small town. At 11 a.m. on 17 January 1887, the Revd Ansel Bourne of Coventry, Rhode Island, drew 551 dollars from a bank in Providence. He paid certain bills and got into a Pawtucket horse-car. This is the last incident he remembers. He did not return home that day, and nothing was heard of him for two months. He was published in the papers as being missing and, foul play being suspected, the police sought his whereabouts in vain.

At seven in the morning of 14 March, however, at Norristown, Pennsylvania, a man calling himself A. J. Brown, who had rented a small shop six weeks previously, stocked it with stationery, confectionery, fruit and sundries, and carried on his quiet trade without seeming to anyone unnatural or eccentric, woke up in a fright and called to the people of the house to tell him where he was. He said his name was Ansel Bourne, that he was ignorant of Norristown, that he knew nothing of shopkeeping, and that the last thing he remembered – it seemed only yesterday – was drawing 551 dollars from the Providence bank. He would not believe that two months had gone by.

The other boarders thought him insane, and so, at first, did Dr Louis H. Reed, whom they called in to see him at three o'clock. But on telegraphing to Providence, confirmatory messages came, and presently his nephew, Mr Andrew Harris, arrived upon the scene, made everything straight, and took him home to Coventry. He was very weak, having apparently lost over twenty pounds of flesh during his escapade, and he had such a horror of the idea of the candy-store that he refused to set foot in one again.

Brown was described by the neighbours as a little taciturn, but in no way odd, and the children of the neighbourhood seemed especially fond of him, for he often doled out free candy. As for

Bourne, his reputation for uprightness was such in the community that no one who knew him could for a moment admit the possibility of his case not being entirely genuine.

In 1890, Ansel Bourne was hypnotized by William James. Bourne knew nothing of Brown, but under trance gave a coherent account of what his other personality had done for the two months lost from Bourne's existence. Wherever his statements could be checked by objective enquiry, they were found to be true.

I am fascinated by the proper names in this account, said Wittgenstein. 'Providence' and 'Coventry' are most appropriate. 'Bourne' is especially resonant, recalling the lines from Hamlet's 'To be or not to be' soliloquy, in which death is addressed as *The undiscovered country from whose bourn / No traveller returns* . . . You might say Bourne had crossed that frontier without knowing he had done so.

Here Wittgenstein concluded his narrative, said Fr Brown.

56

SARDONYX

All this while Fr Brown's eyes had a faraway look, as if interven-
ing in the past; perhaps, if I could see myself, my eyes, too,
would have that look, as I cast my mind back through the decades
to where Maeterlinck and I sat before the fire that All Souls'
night in 1959, listening to his recollections. The clock began to
strike eleven; Fr Brown came to, like one startled out of sleep.

Ah, the forward-flowing tide of time! he cried. How it sweeps
all before it, defying our every effort to recount past times! For
behind every story lies another story, and I have found myself
diverted at every turn in my attempt to give you a biography of
Wittgenstein. In doing so, I am prompted by memory, which St
Augustine likens to a vast field or a spacious palace, a storehouse
for countless images of all kinds.

When I use my memory, he says, I ask it to produce whatever
it is I wish to remember; no sooner do I say, how shall I relate
this, or that, than the images of all the things whereof I wish to
speak spring forward from the same great treasure-house. I open

the portals of my inward eye and stalk the cloisters of my memory, in which images appear at every archway, every alcove, every pillar. Statues manifest themselves at every step, pointing with their eyes or hands towards other graven images; I open another door, and dormant sounds reverberate within the chambers of my ear. Another room has niches stocked with jars made of precious stones – chrysoprase, carnelian, the milky blue of sardonyx, and many more, each memorable for its colour, each holding a specific perfume, redolent of long-forgotten episodes.

As for Wittgenstein's account of Bourne's life, its salient dates imply other narratives not unrelated to the circumstances. These, too, long to be recounted. Thus, 28 October, when Bourne publicly confessed his atheism, is the feast day of St Jude, the patron of hopeless cases; 11 November, when he announced his conversion, that of St Martin of Tours, patron of drunkards, and of tailors; and 15 November, when he proclaimed the return of his faculties, that of St Leopold, duke and patron of Austria, who founded the monastery of Klosterneuberg, where Wittgenstein himself had laboured as a gardener in the summer of 1920. But, to paraphrase Wittgenstein, whereof we have not time to speak, thereof we must remain silent.

Nevertheless, I would urge you to study the lives of these saints for yourselves. You will find our library has large reserves of such material. In fact, you may regard this as an imposition. The other boys of your class are aware that I have summoned you to my office, and they will expect you to return to them complaining of the punishment I have meted out to you. When you tell them that it consists of long drawn-out periods of mental exercise, rather than immediate physical pain, they will be most impressed. Were you to tell them the whole truth about our encounter, you might very probably be taken for teacher's pets, and we would not like that to happen. Say nothing about the tea and Jaffa Cakes. You will present yourselves here after evening chapel a week from today and give me an account of your researches. Now, it is well past your bedtime. I will see you to your dormitory.

It had been a long day. When Maeterlinck and I got into our beds, we fell asleep almost immediately. I dreamed about the library.

57

PARCHMENT

I am standing in an alcove of the library, scanning a book by the light of a mullioned window. The old glass is full of bobbles and dimples, and blips of prismatic light tremble on the pages. When I find the magic word I've been looking for, I utter it and close the book with a bang. A puff of dust hangs for a moment in the air and, as it sifts lazily downwards in the golden light, I realize the power of the word has already begun to take effect.

I find I can lift the books from the shelves without touching them. I extend a telekinetic hand towards them. One by one, they glide out from the bays and stacks and cubicles, hovering spine upwards, their covers fluttering, drifting along the laddered aisles and corridors, congregating at the intersections, some already arriving from the annexes and lower levels, shaking off the dust of centuries, creaking their leather-bound wings, all homing in on me, who am their saviour, for there is a cold war going on beyond the library walls, and they are burning books in the public squares.

I summon them up from the deep wells of knowledge, tomes that were bound by chains to presses and lecterns and carrels, in dungeons lit by remote beams of light from high peepholes and lancets, codices that languished in dark vaults, scrolls that had been sealed in beehive cells in catacombs, bursting from their prisons, chattering and whirring up balustraded staircases through high gaunt halls strewn with torn brocades and moth-eaten tapestries. They flock around me in principalities and powers, ranked in angelic squadrons, awaiting my command to fly out and bomb the city with a million megatons of words.

The real library's dimensions were not so extensive, but were complicated by the ramifications of the catalogue, which defied most accepted principles of taxonomy. For instance, standard multi-volume sets of the *Lives of the Saints*, such as those by Butler and Baring-Gould, could be found in their proper hagiological niche, but, more often than not, book-length studies of specific saints would be filed according to their subject's attributes or patronage. Thus, St Barbara came under Pyrotechnics, St Lucy under Ophthalmology, and St Francis Xavier under Sport, since it is recorded that he had been a keen pelota player in his youth. Moreover, the system rarely accorded to the actual placement of books on the shelves, since generations of librarians had successively, but only partially, upgraded both catalogue and shelving arrangements to fit current strategies of access, so that finding a book was like mining geological strata.

Maeterlinck and I spent much of the first day dipping through the standard *Lives*, and then began a random search which soon revealed the truly idiosyncratic nature of the system. The category of Angelology looked most promising: when we went to the relevant location, we immediately came upon a book which seemed readily assignable to that domain: Gustav Fechner's *Comparative Anatomy of the Angels*, first published in Leipzig in 1825. Briefly, Fechner follows the curve of evolution of the animal kingdom, from the amoeba to man and then, by extrapolation, attempts to construct the ideal form of a still higher being, an angel. He concludes that such a being must be spherical, having evolved from a brain that had become too luminous for its body, which it subsequently abandoned, since it perceived universal gravitation in the same way as human beings perceive light. The angels also communicate by means of light, since they lack vocal equipment.

This was all well and good. However, immediately beside the *Comparative Anatomy*, we found two books whose relation to their neighbour seemed problematic: the Revd William Plumer's *Mary Reynolds of Pennsylvania: Two Souls in One Body*, and *The Mirror of Al-Ghazalī*, author anonymous.

58

INDIAN WHITE

Mary Reynolds, the daughter of the Revd William Reynolds, was born in Lichfield, England, and was a child when the family emigrated to the United States. They settled near Titusville, Pennsylvania; this was still remote frontier country, inhabited mainly by Indians and a few white traders. Wild beasts roamed freely. In the spring of 1811, at the age of about nineteen, Mary went into the woods with a book in her hand. She was not seen again until two days later, when she was discovered lying by a spring well, having seemingly lost consciousness. The book was nowhere to be found. She came to after some hours, but remained apparently blind and deaf for seven weeks, whereupon her hearing returned suddenly; her sight was only restored gradually.

Three months later, she was found in a deep sleep from which she could not be wakened for many hours. When she did awake, she had lost all memory, and was incapable of the most basic speech. Her condition was like that of a new-born infant. However, she soon regained her former capabilities, and within six weeks it was noticed that her facility for language had now far outstripped that of her former self. The original Mary had been quiet, religious, sober to the point of being dull, and rarely spoke except when spoken to. The new Mary was a changed person: cheerful, gay, flirtatious, given to practical jokes, with a remarked talent for impromptu versification; indeed, she often spoke in rhyme without knowing she had done so. She also exhibited some symptoms of echolalia.

Five weeks later, she woke up one morning in her first state, and expressed surprise at the change of seasons, unaware that anything abnormal had happened to her. Four weeks later, she again fell into her second state, and took up life precisely where she had left it some time before; these alternations continued for some fifteen or sixteen years. The two Marys' handwriting were entirely different. The first Mary's was a crabbed minuscule; that of the second Mary, an extravagant copperplate. Both Marys grew to know that the other existed, and were afraid of lapsing into the other's state, for the first considered the second to be bold and forward, while the second thought the first dull and stupid.

At the age of thirty-five, Mary woke up in the second state, in which she remained permanently until her death on 16 October 1854.

The Mirror of Al-Ghazalī bore on the verso of the title page a quotation attributed to St Gregory of Nyssa: *A well-crafted mirror reflects on its polished surface whatever is placed before it: so the soul, when it has left the perishable body, receives in its purity the image of incorruptible beauty.*

On the facing recto the following passage appeared:

In the autumn of 1854 a certain gentleman of about thirty-five was walking in London in the vicinity of St Paul's church. He met a stranger who first invited him to dinner and then suggested that they visit the top of the dome of St Paul's. There, the stranger pulled something like a compass out of his pocket, which subsequently turned out to be a magic mirror. He proposed that the gentleman might see in it anyone he wished, no matter the distance that separated them; and, thinking of his sick father, the gentleman immediately saw him reclining in his armchair in the drawing-room of his home in Edinburgh. Seized with terror, he suggested to his companion that they descend forthwith. But on taking leave, the stranger said to him, Remember, you are the slave of the man in the mirror, and will be until death sets you free.

The rest of the pages of *The Mirror of Al-Ghazalī* were blank.

59

YELLOW PAGES YELLOW

On the second day I made an unexpected discovery. After many hours, I had finally tracked down a book-length account of St Jude, the first of the saints assigned to us by Fr Brown. As I lifted it from its shelf, I saw that another book seemed to have been lodged into the space behind it. It was a thick loose-leaf album bound in yellow cloth, divided into three sections of colour-coded pages, yellow, blue and green. It bore no title. The text, written in various hands in black ink, was further divided up into sections preceded by numerals, in the manner of a mathematical proposition. I flicked through the yellow section; then I began to read more slowly, and with increasing uneasiness, as I realized the nature of what I had stumbled on, as witnessed by these extracts:

1.3 The subject, hereafter referred to as 'Y', identified in St Malachy's Home for Orphan Boys in Belfast, aged two and three months. Exhibited poor hand-to-eye coordination.

Speech not yet progressed beyond an infant babble. It was observed that a candle placed in a room from which all draughts had been rigorously excluded would flicker when 'Y' was introduced. Other minor telekinetic phenomena were reported.

1.14 'Y' is aged four. He claims his guardian angel frequently manifests himself to him. Says his name is Aziz. 'Y' carries on conversations with him, and generally relates to him as he would to a superior playmate.

3.22 Aged seven, 'Y' exhibits higher than normal REM activity. When wakened from a dream, he is inclined to behave as if still participating in the dream, and is able to give a coherent commentary on its actions. Sometimes he includes his observers as characters in the plot, addressing them as Rumpelstiltskin, Rupert, Mickey Mouse, etc., as he deems appropriate. Exhibits minor to fair telekinesis, but has no awareness of his powers, attributing such phenomena to angelic intervention.

3.37 Diminished telekinesis amply compensated for by rapid verbal progress. Aged seven, has reading age of thirteen. Progressive myopia allied to increased inner visualization. Encouraged by guardian, has taken up philately, and is able to detect minor flaws with the naked eye. Guardian acquires subject 'X'.

4.1 'Y' aged eight years and three months. Major breakthrough. When presented with a colour reproduction of van Eyck's *Rolin Madonna*, he was immediately engrossed by it. After half an hour, the wings of the angel were observed to flicker momentarily, and the flowers on the balcony swayed for an instant as if blown by a breeze. The ferry in the distant riverscape moved a fraction of an inch to the left. When 'Y' withdrew his gaze from the image, these effects ceased.

4.11 Private showing of *Rolin Madonna* arranged by courtesy of M——, an alumnus of the Collège de Ste-Barbe, Ghent, and Director of Netherlandish Art at the Louvre, Paris. Maximum security provided. 'Y' given a 2 ml. per litre solution of S.T. in a glass of lemonade. Almost immediately, the angel's wings began to flutter; the angel placed the crown on the head of the Madonna. Observing this, the Chancellor Rolin drew back in alarm, knocking his missal to the floor. When 'Y' was blindfolded, the effects took some minutes to subside. 5 ml. solution given intravenously. Noticeable increase in effects.

60

DORIAN GRAY

(Yellow Book, blue pages)

1.2 Eighth 'birthday'. 'Y' given paint-box. Emphasize names of colours: Burnt Sienna, Prussian Blue, Heliotrope, etc., in conjunction with historical & hagiographical detail: Napoleon, St Helena, etc. (cf. Paris Green). Guardian to introduce St Augustine. Story of Hermaphroditus, but edit out graphic detail. Story of green-skinned triplets, two boys and a girl, as per account in van Eyck document. Impress on 'Y' the efficacy of relics.

2.13 9 Feb 1955. Feast of St Apollonia, birthday of Lord Carson. At this stage the Oscar Wilde account might be usefully introduced, especially in relation to Wilde's predilection for gemstones. See passages in *Salome*, e.g.

I have topazes, yellow as are the eyes of tigers, and

topazes that are pink as the eyes of a wood-pigeon, and green topazes that are as the eyes of cats. I have opals that burn always with an ice-blue flame, opals that make sad men's minds, and are fearful of the shadows. I have onyxes like the eyeballs of a dead woman. I have moonstones that change when the moon changes, and are wan when they see the sun. I have sardonyx and hyacinth stones, etc., etc.

2.14 Summarize *The Picture of Dorian Gray*. Compare to Conan Doyle, *The Empty House*:

The shadow of a man who was seated in a chair within was thrown in hard, black outline upon the luminous screen of the window. There was no mistaking the poise of the head, the squareness of the shoulders, the sharpness of the features. The face was turned half-round, and the effect was that of one of those black silhouettes which our grandparents loved to frame. It was a perfect reproduction of Holmes. So amazed was I that I threw out my hand to make sure that the man himself was standing beside me.

3.71 Imagine spaces under the floorboards, between walls. The otherworld of lost things where nothing is ever lost.

3.82 Imagine human beings living in an underground den, which has a mouth open towards the light and reaching all along the den; they have been here since childhood, and have their legs and necks chained so that they cannot move, and can only see before them, being prevented by the chains from turning their heads. Above and behind them a fire is blazing at a distance, and between the fire and the prisoners there is a raised gangway; and you will see, if you look, a low wall built along this gangway, like the screen against which puppet-masters operate their puppets.

I see.

And do you see, I said, men passing along the wall carrying all sorts of vessels, and statues and figures of animals made of wood and stone and various materials, which appear over the wall? Some of them are talking, others silent.

You have shown me a strange image, and they are strange prisoners.

Like ourselves, I replied.

7.19 OPERATION OF THE TIMEBELT: Theory and Relations; Time Tracking; The Paradox Paradox; Alternity; Discoursing; Protections; Corrections; Tangling and Excising; Excising with Records; Reluctances; Avoidances and Responsibilities.

7.20 FUNCTIONS: Layout and Controls; Settings; Compound Settings; High-Order Programming; Safety Features.

61

GALLAHER'S GREEN

(Yellow Book, green pages)

3.4 16 October 1874 (Feast of St Gall, twentieth birthday of Oscar Wilde). Fr Gerard Hopkins visits National Gallery. Sees Arnolfini portrait. Notes in his Journal 'deeps of transparent colour', reminding him of a Turkish rug in a room used for chapel, where the blue and green seemed to stand in higher tufts than the red. Similar illusion with blue window-glass. Further compares Arnolfini colours to gemstones in National History Museum, visited earlier that day: 'beryl, watery green; carnelian, Indian red; chrysoprase, beautiful half-transparent green; sardonyx, milky blue flake in bloom'.

18.23 24 July 1959. Christina the Astonishing. Guardian discusses aspects of philately with 'Y'. Mauritius Blue.

Introduces 'Y' to photographic tints. Relates story of death of Absalom, son of David, II Samuel 19. Explains that the 'oak' of the story is the terebinth tree, from whence comes turpentine:

> *And Absalom met the servants of David. And Absalom rode upon a mule, and the mule went under the thick boughs of a great oak, and his head caught hold of the oak, and he was taken up between the heavens and the earth: and the mule that was under him went away.*

i.e. compare to oil paint invented by van Eyck (oak); suspension of pigment in turpentine, etc.

Guardian shows 'Y' portrait of 'X' as Cleopatra. Asp etc.:
Age cannot wither her, nor custom stale / Her infinite variety.
Also *My salad days, when I was green in judgement.*

18.24 Batch of S.T., as best as our chemists can prepare, delivered. A.M.D.G. A.O.H.

19.1 'X' & 'Y' quite familiar. (See Green Book, 18.17.) Suitable outfit for 'X': plain bottle-green pleated skirt; red cable-knit cardigan with leather buttons; off-white (magnolia?) blouse; white ankle socks, brown daisy-punched sandals; butterfly clasp in hair. Supply Gallaher's 'Greens'. Examine suitability of Waterworks site.

19.9 Gallaher's 'Greens' injected with 2 ml. solution. Waterworks venue found satisfactory. 'X' & 'Y' meet at dusk; guardian maintains unaware state. 'X' & 'Y' climb the railings and begin to walk around the Lower Reservoir. A pale moon is rising, reflected in the waters as swans glide over it. There is a scent of foxglove in the air, and the perfume of woodsmoke drifts down from the woods of Cave Hill. 'X' and 'Y' climb to the Upper Reservoir. Here the moon is reflected too. Reeds are stippled in their own reflection. Next night, they smoke 'Greens'. All day it has been threatening thunder. They reach the Upper Reservoir. The night air oozes damp & heavy with ozone & foxglove scent. They lie down on the little stony beach beyond the old swimming-platform. It begins to pour, warm splashy drops, etc., etc.

62

POWDER PINK

I shut the book, trembling. For all its lacunae, its sometimes feeble grasp of chronology, its slipshod description, for all its shabbily objective voice, there could be no doubt about it: the Yellow Book was a portrait of myself. I had just looked into its crooked mirror.

I remember now gazing at my face sometimes in the wash-bowl mirror in the morning, wondering who this bleary stranger was who could not look me properly in the eye. At other times, it was as if I had been newly born and saw the world with the clear uncomprehending vision of a child. Was this, then, me? This boy was beginning to get a down on his upper lip.

I thought back: now I remembered the Waterworks that night. How could I have forgotten? We had swum out into the broad dark pond as the storm plashed heavily into the water. We moved in an element of water, seeming to breathe water, gulping it in in mouthfuls from the downpouring air. Underneath was a cool green gloom. The sky was shimmering with lightning: I saw her face in pale glimpses.

We were swimming in the deep pool at the lock gate when a lightning bolt hit the gate and burst it asunder. A solid wall of water rushed out and hit us face-on. We were hammered into the pool, pummelled beneath it by the force of the wave. Black and blue, bruised yellow water becoming bottle green on contact. We sank down in each other's arms.

Then my mind went blank.

I tried to clear my head. I had come across no mention of my mother in the book. I had been brought up to believe that my father had died before I was born, but I realized I knew nothing of his life, nor what he had done in it. But my mother? I could still smell her perfume, the pink aroma of her powder compact. I could see the compact itself, and the scallop design on its lid. I remembered dressing up at Hallowe'en in her clothes, the swish of her silk gown, the fox fur draped around my neck, and the ache in my instep arches, as I teetered along in her high heels down streets clouded by the smoke of squibs and bonfires. I decided to look into the Yellow Book again.

Yellow pages, **7.8**. Street photograph of mother and 'Y' in Royal Avenue, Belfast, outside Robinson & Cleaver's department store. It is high summer, 1952: both subjects are squinting into the lens. He is wearing: hand-knitted grey wool sleeveless pullover, cream shirt, plain red tie, hand-knitted grey knee-socks, brown crepe-soled sandals. She:

bottle-green velvet round-brimmed hat with green-tinted
feather, navy heather-fleck box jacket, just below knee-
length pencil-line matching skirt, seamed flesh-toned nylon
stockings, single-strap wedge-heeled navy shoes. Street
traffic: trams, trolleybuses, occasional black motor cars, a
brewer's dray. Memory of beer and horse-dung, petrol
fumes. Warm smell of mother's skirt, cool feel of her hand
on his. The photographer towers over 'Y', the camera
obscuring his whole face. He is wearing a brown felt hat,
single-breasted navy pin-stripe suit, white shirt frayed at the
collar, indeterminate tie. After the photograph is taken he
winks confidentially at 'Y'. Turning to mother, he doubles
back the left lapel of his jacket, to momentarily flash a brass
stick-pin in the shape of a harp supported by two shamrocks.
He gives mother his card. Mother rummages in handbag.
Does she pay him there and then, or not? He retracts the
bellows of the camera, snibs it shut, turns on his heel and
vanishes into the crowd.

63

HOOKER'S GREEN

8.13 Mother's handbag: shoulder-strapped, green mock crocodile skin, slightly scuffed at the edges, with an intertwining snakelike metal clasp. Contents: rouge, lipstick, nail-scissors, etc., a small mirror-backed hairbrush, a tortoiseshell comb, a red leather diary with a miniature pencil in its spine, a Belfast Corporation gas bill, a plastic vial of Lourdes water in the shape of a figurine of the Virgin Mary, with a blue coronet stopper; a brown leather accordion-pleated loose-change purse containing a crumpled ten-shilling note, two half-crowns, three florins, five shilling pieces, four sixpences, five threepenny bits, nine pennies, three ha'pennies, and one farthing, making a total of £1/10/1¼; a pair of rosary beads in a mother-of-pearl case, a sewing kit, a box of Parma Violets, three Miraculous Medals attached to a safety-pin, a knitting pattern for a Fair Isle sweater, folded in four, a string of artificial pearls, a holy picture of St Lucy proffering a pair

of eyes on a saucer, five loose buttons, and a street
photograph of mother and child, taken outside Robinson &
Cleaver's department store in the summer of 1952.

11.2 Mannequins in Ladies' and Men's Clothing
departments come alive at night. The next morning, staff
find several males in Ladies', and vice versa, poised in
correctly arrested attitudes, but with clothing slightly
dishevelled. Minor item in local newspapers.

11.17 Somnambule routine: one morning 'Y' is told he has
been sleepwalking again last night. Emphasize 'again'.
Describe symptoms: eyes wide open, conversation
conducted normally, etc., but bearing no relationship to
current reality: he believed he was in a department store.
When it was suggested to him that he test one of the beds in
the Home Furnishings department, he returned upstairs to
his own bed. Sample of automatic writing, in 'Y's hand.
Gibberish.

12.3 Writing-cabinet, drawer (2): brass pocket compass,
alloy cigarette-case, both engraved with father's name &
harp & two shamrocks motif, blank postcard (hand-tinted)
showing St James's shrine in Santiago de Compostela,
photograph of mother & father & guardian, curved briar
pipe with amber mouthpiece almost bitten through,
miscellaneous foreign coins, a Hooker's Green crayon-stub,
a plastic magnifying glass with scuffed lens.

13.4 Pocket edition of R. L. Stevenson, *Island Nights Entertainments*, in dark mauve grained leatherette, with facsimile RLS autograph in gold on front cover, marbled endpapers, illustrated by 'Nick', with an introduction by Patrick Braybrooke, British Books, London, n.d., dogeared at p. 160 of 'The Bottle Imp':

'I must explain to you there is a peculiarity about the bottle. Long ago, when the devil brought it first upon earth, it was extremely expensive, and was sold first of all to Prester John for many millions of dollars; but it cannot be sold at all, unless sold at a loss. If you sell it for as much as you paid for it, back it comes to you like a homing pigeon. It follows that the price has kept falling in these centuries, and the bottle is now remarkably cheap. I bought it myself from one of my great neighbours on this hill, and the price I paid was only ninety dollars. I could sell it for as high as eighty-nine dollars and ninety-nine cents, but not a penny dearer, or back the thing must come to me. Now, about this there are two bothers. First, when you offer a bottle so singular for eighty-odd dollars, people suppose you to be jesting. And second – but there is no hurry about that – and I need not go into it. Only remember it must be coined money that you sell it for.'

'How am I to know that this is all true?' asked Keawe.

64

CLERICAL PURPLE

As I read these words, I heard a footfall at my back, and turned around in some alarm. It was Maeterlinck. He was pale as a ghost, and he held a book bound in blue cloth.

I found it behind a life of St Martin of Tours, he whispered.

Blue pages, **5.5**. 'A queer thing is a mirror; a picture frame that holds hundreds of different pictures, all vivid and vanished forever.' G. K. Chesterton, 'The Mirror of the Magistrate'.

7.3 'Z' at Oostacker: striped one-piece navy & white bathing-costume covering chest & upper thighs, broad-brimmed straw hat, open-toed sandals, knuckle of right big toe skinned. He has just been swimming in the canal, and is reclining on a deck-chair (faded pink & green striped canvas). It is hot; steam rises from his garment. Paradoxical sensation: goosefleshed limbs, warm and cold at the same time. He drowses amid the sound of his guardian's bees. Blue and yellow hives of the bees. Guardian looming over him in beekeeper's hat and veil.

8.18 Ghent, St Bavon altarpiece: good results.

8.19 Rue du Canard, Rue des Foulons, Rue des Baguettes, Rue du Paradis, Rue Plateau, Rue de la Coriandre, Rue du Chantier, Rue du Moulin à Foulon, Rue d'Or, Rue du Bonheur, Rue de Bruges, Rue aux Ours, Rue des Peignes, Rue des Épingles, Rue des Balais, Rue de la Corne, Rue du Bac, Pont du Pain Perdu, Pont aux Herbes, Pont du Lavage, Rue des Deux Ponts, Rue du Soleil, Rue du Jardin, Porte aux Vaches, Place van Eyck, Rue du Lama, Rue des Riches Claires, Rue des Juifs, Rue des Apôtres, Rue de la Tour Rouge, Rue aux Fleurs, Rue de la Vallée, Rue des Douze Chambres, Rue des Boutiques, Rue du Cumin, Rue de la Farine, Rue Courte d'Argent, Rue Longue de la Vigne, Rue de Repentir, Rue Sel, Rue de la Carpe, Rue des Pilots, Rue du Tigre, Rue de la Rosarie, Rue de l'Éléphant, Rue des Prêtres, Rue des Maçons, Rue des Femmes, Rue des Nonnes Anglaises, Rue du Prince, Rue de l'Étoile d'Or, Rue de l'Épine, Rue du Miroir.

8.21 Ghent, which is not unfitly surnamed 'La Ville de Flore', has a speciality for horticulture, and annually exports whole cargoes of camellias, azaleas, laurel-trees, palms, and other hothouse plants.

8.22 Bruges 1525: Merchant quarters: counting houses, consular palaces & offices of Spain, Florence, Bordeaux, England, Scotland, Ireland, Hamburg, Venice, Bilbao, Portugal. Best hats in the world are made in Bruges. Markets: English wool, lead, tin, cheese. Norwegian gerfalcons & butter; Danish pigs & palfreys; Russian wax & furs; Spanish saffron, mercury, oranges & figs; opium & rugs from Fez; Irish lard, oak & hides; Armenian carpets.

8.23 Ludwig Wittgenstein, *Tractatus Logico-Philosophicus*. 2.063 The total reality is the world. 2.1 We make to ourselves pictures of facts. 2.16 In order to be a picture a fact must have something in common with what it pictures.

9.1 Meaningful coincidences are thinkable as pure chance. But the more they multiply and the greater and more exact the correspondence is, the more their probability sinks and their unthinkability increases, until they can no longer be regarded as pure chance . . .

65

HYDE GREEN

(Blue Book, yellow pages)

2.31 Rue du Poivre:

> *I speak severely to my boy,*
> *I beat him when he sneezes;*
> *For he can thoroughly enjoy*
> *The pepper when he pleases!*

Here, you may nurse it a bit, if you like! said the
Duchess to Alice, flinging the baby at her as she spoke.

3.37 The Bee. Key to Folding Model. The Queen Bee (on
left). Plate I (Upper side) Head, thorax and abdomen from
above. 1 – Labella. 2 – Labial palps. 3 – Upper jaw or
mandible. 4 – Clypeus. 5 – Upper lip or labrum. 6 – Scape
of antennae. 7 – Flagellum of antennae. 8 – Ocelli or simple

eyes. 9 – Compound eyes. 10 – Front leg. 11 – Middle leg. 12 – Hind leg. 13 – Hooks or hamuli of hind wing. 14 – Hamular fold of fore wing. 15 – Tergum of thorax. 16 – A single tergite or dorsal plate of one of the abdominal segments. 17 – Apex of abdomen. Plate I (Under side) Respiratory system and heart. 18 – Breathing holes (stigmata). 19 – Air sacs. 20 – Aorta. 21 – Folds in the aorta. 22 – Ventricles of heart. 23 – Abdomen.

3.48 Rocking horse, Rue du Poivre: Z considers the horse's head from all angles: flared air-intakes of the nostrils; nose-cone of the nose; spirit-level-bubble eyes; throttle of the throat; radar ears. Joystick of the reins. Stirrup-controlled ailerons of the retractable wings. Saddle ejector-seat. Pillowcase parachute.

6.66 He thanked me with a smiling nod, measured out a few minims of the red tincture and added one of the powders. The mixture, which was at first of a reddish hue, began, in proportion as the crystals melted, to brighten in colour, to effervesce audibly, and to throw off small fumes of vapour. Suddenly and at the same moment, the ebullition ceased and the compound changed to a dark purple, which faded again more slowly to a watery green.

7.1. After Aladdin had feasted heartily on these good things, they rose up, and went on their walk, crossing many gardens and fine meadows, the magician all the while telling a number of amusing stories. At length they arrived at the beginning of a narrow valley bounded on each side by lofty and bare mountains.

7.3 He took the lamp which stood lighted in the niche, extinguished it, and put it in the bosom of his shirt. On his way back through the garden he stopped to look more carefully at the fruit, which he had only glanced at before. The fruit of each tree had a separate colour. Some were white, others sparkling and transparent; some were red; others green, blue and violet; some of a yellowish hue; in short, there were fruits of almost every colour. The white were pearls; the sparkling and transparent fruit were diamonds; the deep red were rubies; the green, emeralds; the blue, turquoises; the violet, amethysts; those tinged with yellow, sapphires. All were of the largest size, and the most perfect ever seen in the world; but Aladdin thought they were only pieces of coloured glass.

13.7 Matthew 6:22. *The light of the body is in the eye.*

13.8 The blind Swiss naturalist François Huber built the first 'leaf hive', of 12 frames hinged at the back; for observation, this 'book' could be opened to the desired leaf, & studied.

13.9 I say unto you, look around and survey the fabric of the universe. *The Golden Legend.*

66

LILAC HAZE

(Blue Book, green pages)

2.12 Air Liner. Key to Folding Model. Fuselage. 1 – Nose of Machine. 2 – Compensating Gear. 3 – Instrument Boards. 4 – Chief Pilot. 5 – Chief Pilot's Control Wheel turned right and left operating ailerons; pushed fore and aft controlling elevators. 6 – Second Pilot. 7 – Second Pilot's Control Wheel coupled with Chief Pilot's Control, forming Dual Control. 8 – Cables to Ailerons. 9 – Engine Controls (four in number). 10 – Chief Pilot's Rudder Bar, controlling Rudder. 11 – 2nd Pilot's Rudder Bar. 12 – Enclosed Pilot's Cockpit. 13 – Bulkhead. 14 – Wireless Operator's Cabin. 15 – Wireless Operator. 16 – Aerial Tube. 17 – Wireless Aerial let out and trailing in the wind when machine is in flight. 18 – Forward Passenger Cabin. 19 – Luggage Rack with front rail forming ventilating pipe. 20 – Interior decorated with sound insulating material to prevent noises reaching passengers. 21 – Bulkhead. 22 – Corridor. 23 – Luggage and Mails Compartment. 24 – Lavatories. 25 – Stewards' Bar. 26 – Refreshment Room. 27 – After Saloon and Smoking Compartments. 28 – Passengers smoking cigarettes. 29 – Tubular Frame Work of after end of Fuselage. 30 – Tail Landing Wheel. 31 – Tail Planes or Empennage.

5.71 Mirror sb. [ME. *mirour* – O Fr. *mirour* (mod. *miroir*) – Rom. *miratorium*, f. *mirat–*, pa. ppl. stem of L. *mirari, –are* wonder, look at]
2. spec. **a.** A magic glass or crystal ME. **b.** A small glass formerly worn in the hat by men and at the girdle by women. B. JONS.

5.73 Parrot sb. 1525. [prob. appellative use of Fr †*Perrot* (cf. PIERROT), dim. of *Pierre* Peter; *pérot* is given by Littré as a familiar name in mod. Fr. for the bird, and *pierrot* for house-sparrow; cf. PARAKEET.]

6.1 Bird cage: trapeze; little round mirror; bowls for seed & water, etc. Dympna the parrot pecks at her face in the mirror. Dympna, Dympna. Uncle Franck: Beagle Green dress jacket with Blackberry lapels, Delft Rose velvet waistcoat with gold rose & thorn pattern, Lilac Haze silk shirt with cutaway collar, Aconite Violet dress tie with Amulet Green stick-pin, Arabian Blue trousers, Forget-me-not socks. His shoes still remain in the wardrobe. Dympna! Dympna!

9.9 There was no mirror, at that date, in my room; that which stands beside me as I write, was brought there later on and for the very purpose of these transformations. That night, however, was far gone into the morning – the morning, black as it was, was nearly ripe for the conception of the day – the inmates of my house were locked in the most rigorous hours of slumber; and I determined, flushed as I was with hope and triumph, to venture in my new shape as far as to my bedroom. I crossed the yard, wherein the constellations looked down upon me, I could have thought, with wonder, the first creature of that sort that their unsleeping vigilance had yet disclosed to them; I stole through the corridors, a stranger in my own house; and coming to my room, I saw for the first time the appearance of Edward Hyde.

9.11 I was told that we do evil because we choose to do so of our own free will, and suffer it because your justice rightly demands that we should. I did my best to understand this, but I could not see it clearly. I tried to raise my mental perceptions out of the abyss which engulfed them, but I sank back into it once more. Again and again I tried; but always I sank back. One thing lifted me up into the light of your day. It was that I knew I had a will, as surely as I knew that there was life in me. I was myself, and not some other person. St Augustine, *Confessions*, VII, 3.

67

BEE GREEN

Maeterlinck and I looked at each other with a wild surmise. The books each contained several hundreds of pages. Though our examination had been cursory, we could see that the entries were not necessarily chronological. Some passages were familiar to us, others were not. If the books were a record, they appeared to have gaps.

What do you think? I asked Maeterlinck.

Last night, said Maeterlinck slowly, I had a dream about my uncle Franck's briefcase. Only when I came across the entry in the Blue Book referring to him did I remember it. The briefcase had a steel lock, very big and square, and very finely constructed. It looked like one of those complicated padlocks one sometimes sees in museums; indeed, the door to the staircase in the Belfry of Ghent has just such a lock. I lacked a key to the lock and was wondering how I might open it, when my uncle Franck's voice spoke from the keyhole. Then I realized that it was a kind of amplifier for a recording machine which was concealed within the briefcase: it was, in fact, an antique phonograph, for I remembered that my uncle Franck had once shown me how to construct a working model of such a device from a cardboard funnel, a membrane made from parchment or greaseproof paper, a bristle from a yard-brush, and a cylinder covered with a thin coating of candlewax: this, he insisted, must be beeswax, for it was most sympathetic to vibrations.

Uncle Franck's voice, as it emerged feebly from the keyhole, trembled and hesitated, fading behind a background noise, as if the briefcase also contained a swarm of bees. I was therefore reluctant to open it; but Franck's voice sounded so pitiful that I felt I had no option. I gathered that the lock had not been locked at all; I had only to unsnib the latch. This I did and, as I opened the briefcase, the bees emerged and swarmed all over my body. They were no ordinary bees: they were coloured blue and yellow, lapis lazuli and gold, and as they whirled around me, I became the bees, or they became me. I glimpsed myself in the mirror: I had become a spinning wraith, composed of blue and yellow molecules. Faster and faster we spun, the colours merging, till they became a haze of green.

I was about to fly like smoke up the chimney, out across the rooftops, when I woke up to find myself in my bed in Loyola House. This dream must have a bearing on our circumstances. What do you think it means?

Blue and yellow together make green, I replied. I remember when I first witnessed this alchemy as a child. I believe it is referred to in the Yellow Book. I can still smell the different aromatic weights of the paints, of plasticine and chalk-dust, and sour milk. I can see my schoolteacher, Miss Taggart: she is wearing a leopardskin blouse, and because of this I think of her as Miss Tiger. But she is not at all fierce. I am painting on coarse charcoal-coloured paper that has little wisps of other colours in it, and the brush makes a scratchy sound against it. Beneath a blue sky and a yellow sun I paint a house with a green door, and a green garden dotted with blue and yellow flowers.

Blue and yellow make green. I remember a mention of a Green Book in the Yellow Book. Perhaps this Green Book is the key. We must walk through the green door.

Before long we found the book, behind a life of Leopold of Austria, just as we had expected.

68

DOLL'S EYE BLUE

(Green Book, yellow pages)

3.17 They are taken into cots, dragged into the heavy folds of illness, present in dreams, involved in the fatalities of night fevers; yet they possess only rudimentary knowledge. They are fed imaginary food, for their lips cannot be forced apart. Perhaps they only allow themselves to be dreamed, for they are only fully awake when they sleep with their too-big eyes wide open. When everyone around us answered us by pointing out the names for things, they were the first to question us with silence.

3.19 There is a moment when the loops and curlicues begin to move by themselves, unfolding slowly across the landscape page like smoke trailed from an aeroplane. As the words are whispered in the inner ear, their conformations emerge visibly, and the fact becomes a picture. The white of

the ink-well speckled with blue. 'X' is learning how to
write. To begin, she copies the letters she reads off the
writing-book.

6.81 'X' has boxes for trinkets, for buttons, for pencils, for
chalks, for holy pictures, for medals, for books. There are
boxes inside boxes. Every day, she rearranges the contents of
the boxes, making mental labels for them. But the ghosts of
what were there before remain, like faint perfumes, and
when she opens up a box she feels an odour of the past waft
over her, and the buttons, suddenly disclosed, take on the
faces of holy medals.

7.23 She is six when she first sees the statue of the Virgin
move. It is evening Benediction. The Virgin nods her head in
the trembling candle-light. When 'X' realizes this, the
Virgin smiles.

7.39 The basic function of each being is expanding and
contracting. Expanded beings are permeative; contracted
beings are dense and impermeative. Therefore each of us,
alone or in combination, may appear as space, energy or mass,
depending on the ratio of expansion to contraction chosen,
and what kind of vibrations each of us expresses by alternating
expansion and contraction. Each being controls his or her own
vibrations. The universe is an infinite harmony of vibrating
beings in an elaborate range of expansion–contraction ratios,
frequency modulations, and so forth.

11.1 She sees the noble soul of the rocking-horse. Rider and steed have flown over Arabia. He teaches her to fly so they can be equals. When he dies, for he must die when she grows up, she will fly by herself.

13.3 The night came like the turning out of a lamp, and in another moment came tomorrow. The laboratory grew faint and hazy, then fainter and ever fainter. Tomorrow night came black, then day again, night again, day again, faster and faster still. An eddying murmur filled my ears, and a strange, dumb confusedness descended on my mind.

13.7 USAGES: Forward in time – by a Specific Amount, to a Particular Moment; Cautions; Additional Cautions; Fail-Safe Functions; Compound Cautions; Compound Jumps, Advanced & High Order; Distance Jumps, including Ultra Long Range; Special Cautions, including Infinity Dangers & Entropy Awareness; Time-Skimming; Timestop, including Uses of the Timestop, Stopping the Present, Stopping the Past, & Stopping the Future . . .

69

PRIMROSE

(Green Book, blue pages)

1.1 Blue is the deepest colour; unimpeded, the gaze plumbs infinity, the colour forever escaping it. The elusive bird of happiness is blue. Paint the surface of a wall blue, and it is no longer a wall. Blue disembodies. To penetrate the blue is to go through the looking-glass. Blue is the colour of our Lady. It is valid to wear blue at the funerals of children, for they are not yet fully of this world.

4.15 Difficulties with 'X's wardrobe. Sometimes wears Monday's clothes on Tuesdays, and will not accept that Sunday best is not for every day of the week. Demands to choose for herself. But compensated for by increased TK awareness: her dolls, she insists, play by themselves while she sleeps.

4.103 Guardian accidentally knocks 'Mary Jane' to the floor in 'X's presence. A bruise instantly appears on its knee, a graze blossoms on its elbow. 'X' looks away; the wounds fade in a second.

7.4 Arnolfini portrait. Good results. Candle-flame seen to flicker. 'X's face glimpsed briefly in mirror.

11.13 Then she began looking about, and noticed that what could be seen from the old room was quite common and uninteresting, but that all the rest was as different as possible. For instance, the pictures on the wall next to the fire seemed to be all alive, and the very clock on the chimney-piece (you know you can only see the back of it in the Looking-glass) had got the face of an old man, and grinned at her.

12.13 *For they remember yet the tales we told them*
Around the hearth, of fairies long ago,
When they loved still in fancy to behold them
Quick dancing earthward in the feathery snow.

But now the young and fresh imagination
Finds traces of their presence everywhere,
And peoples with a new and bright creation
The clear blue chambers of the sunny air.

13.11 Pressed primrose flower found between pp. 210–211 of *The Fairyland of Science*, by Arabella B. Buckley (London:

Edward Stanford, 26 & 27 Cockspur Street, Charing Cross, S.W., 1899). Turin Shroud Brown imprint of flower on following passage:

We have already pointed out that in our fairy-land of nature all things work together so as to bring order out of apparent confusion. But though we should naturally expect winds and currents, rivers and clouds, and even plants to follow fixed laws, we should scarcely have looked for such regularity in the life of the active, independent busy bee. Yet we see that she, too, has her own appointed work to do, and does it regularly, and in an orderly manner. In this lecture we have been speaking entirely of the bee within the hive, and noticing how marvellously her instincts guide her in her daily life. But within the last few years we have learnt that she performs a most curious and wonderful work in the world outside her home, and that we owe to her not only the sweet honey we eat, but even in a great degree the beauty and gay colours of the flowers which she visits when collecting it. This work will form the subject of our next lecture, and while we love the little bee for her constant industry, patience, and order within the hive, we shall, I think, marvel at the wonderful law of nature which guides her in her unconscious mission of love among the flowers which grow around it.

70

VERDIGRIS

(Green Book, green pages)

1.1 Green is the colour of water, as red is the colour of fire. Green is linked to thunder. Life ascends from red and blossoms in green. Red is a male colour; green, a female colour. Although emeralds are papal jewels, they were also the jewels of Lucifer, before his fall from Heaven. *Emerald delights the eye without fatiguing it*: Pliny. Greenland was discovered by Eric the Red, who felt it could make men's minds long to go there, if it had a fine name. Off-stage, the actors relax in the green room. *A green thought in a green shade*.

3.2 'X' contemplates the red fruit and the green leaves of the cherry tree outside the window of the Arnolfinis' room. The lady, with her big belly, looks like a green queen bee beside the drab man. 'X' drifts into the painting, and out of the window. Under the tree are three beehives: one pink, one yellow, one blue. The grassy garden, bright with blue and yellow flowers, leads down to the edge of an emerald canal, which reflects many-windowed houses, roofs, chimneys, steeples. She floats across a little jade bridge and into the swarming noises of the city.

11.7 Inner sanctum of the darkroom, lit by a dim ruby holy-picture lamp. The second hand sweeps over the luminous blips of the clock as, swimming in developing liquid, the photographic plate blooms with 'X's image, like breath fading from a mirror. Her guardian clips a dripping print to a line with a clothes-pin. Then another. Then another. She remembers other photographs of herself growing smaller back through the years, and thinks of herself being folded up like a telescope.

13.101 Suppose 'X' sees a blue dress in a shop window, and that an hour later she sees a girl in a stationer's shop. In the following night's dreams, she may see the girl wearing the blue dress. Or herself wearing the blue dress. Or her fingers smeared with blue ink from a leaking fountain pen.

17.101 Under the surface verdigris glaze of the woman's green dress are two opaque underlayers, containing verdigris, lead-tin yellow and lead white. Verdigris is manufactured by alchemy, from copper and vinegar. According to Cennino, verdigris mixed with white lead and a little liquid varnish makes a superlative cement for mending broken hourglasses. Verdigris is essential for painting water, or fish, bearing in mind that fish, and all irrational animals, always have shadows on their backs. For an outstanding fish, lace it with a few spines of gold, which will shine nicely through the green medium.

19.9 Some yellow spoons came up with the tumblers after dinner. Somebody said they were brass and I tasted them to find out and it seemed so. Some time afterwards as I came in from a stroll with Mr Purbrick, he told me Hügel had said the scarlet or rose colour of flamingos was found to be due to a fine copper powder on the feathers. As he said this I tasted the brass in my mouth. Fr Hopkins, *Journal*, 10 August 1874. (Feast of St Lawrence, who is invoked against fire; of St Bettelin, who fell in love with an Irish princess; and of St Emygdius, invoked against earthquakes.)

21.9 Jan van Eyck, *Madonna in a Church*. The gigantic Madonna looms as high as the triforium, holding her giant baby in the crook of her right arm. Her robe is a deep Gallaher's Blue: 'X' is smoking a Blue, thinking of the much lighter blue of the smoke. The Virgin's underdress is Clarion Red. In the inner sanctum, the altar is ablaze with candles; Mass is being celebrated by a pair of angels with flamingo wings. Patches of light fallen from the higher windows are dappled on the nave floor: the sun shines from the north. Either that, or its architect deliberately misaligned the church, whose architecture is in any case imaginary, although it contains features visible in some known churches. An inch of ash droops from the end of the Blue; 'X' taps it off into an ash-tray, where it becomes a grey worm.

71

GREEN ROSE

Maeterlinck and I were about to read on, when we heard a foot-fall at our backs. We turned round. Standing before us was my uncle Celestine.

I am here, he said gravely, to offer you an apologia. You have read the books, or rather, you have skimmed them, for to read them properly would take an age; many years have gone into them. And I can see that one might draw all sorts of conclusions from them. But before you do so, let me say that it was important that you came across these books by yourselves, and that you read them with an open mind. You will, of course, have observed that certain passages appear to bear a direct relevance to your-selves; but the books are not mere biographies. Some passages include scenarios that failed to materialize; some describe events as they happened, but not as you remember them; and some are fictions. But all in all, the books contain more truth than other people's memories of themselves, which are constantly revised to suit their current image of themselves.

You are special. We have not moulded you, nor made you in our image. Your free will has not been compromised, for it is essential that you enter our plan with full knowledge and consent.

As St Thomas says, the highest manifestation of life consists in this – that a being governs its own actions. That which is always subject to the direction of another is somewhat of a dead thing. Now a slave does not govern his own actions, but rather they are governed for him. Hence a man in so far as he is a slave is a very image of death.

But you are very much alive, for you have shown yourselves capable of powers beyond those of ordinary mortals. We have observed you closely, that is true, but only as good parents would, to guide your natural gifts and bring them to fruition. In this respect, you are like the bee, which has never been domesticated: man provides her with a superior home, so that she can devote more of her time to making honey. It is, I hope, a fair exchange. The relationship between man and bee is one of mutual respect for each other's temporal dominions.

Once upon a time I was like you, singled out from an early age to be a primary agent of our great mission. Alas! When I attained the use of reason, my embryonic powers began to diminish; the more I learned to read and write, the more the other, extra-sensory world receded from me. Even so, when I was eight I was granted a vision of St Rose of Lima, in which she appeared clothed in a garment made of green roses. When I was nine, I had a vision of a single green rose, which bore St Rose's features; she spoke to me, saying that from now on I would have to make do with the eyes of ordinary mortals. By the time I was ten, the supernatural was invisible to me and I was left as I am, comparatively blind. Yet I, too, serve the cause in my own way, and I am privileged to serve you.

How we three have come to be here, in the library of Loyola House, is the culmination of a long concatenation of events. Let me begin by telling you that in London in 1889 – the year of Ludwig Wittgenstein's birth – Arthur Conan Doyle and Oscar Wilde were introduced to each other at a dinner given by an influential American publisher. The result was that Wilde was commissioned to write *The Portrait of Dorian Gray*, a book in which art and life would become inextricably confused; Doyle's commission was *The Sign of Four*, the novel that would fully establish the character of Sherlock Holmes, who is believed by many to have led an actual, flesh-and-blood existence.

72

THORN PINK

The date of this momentous encounter was 23 August, the feast of St Rose of Lima, who, having entered the Third Order of St Dominic, modelled herself on St Catherine of Siena. Significantly, St Catherine is often depicted holding a book in one hand, and a heart in the other: emblems familiar to Wilde and Doyle, who might be said to be two sides of the same coin. Let us compare the opening passages of the two books commissioned that day.

The Sign of Four:

Sherlock Holmes took his bottle from the corner of the mantel-piece, and his hypodermic syringe from its neat morocco case. With his long, white, nervous fingers he adjusted the delicate needle, and rolled back his left shirt-cuff. For some little time his eyes rested thoughtfully upon the sinewy forearm and wrist, all dotted and scarred with

innumerable puncture-marks. Finally, he thrust the sharp
point home, pressed down the tiny piston, and sank back
into the velvet-lined chair with a long sigh of satisfaction.

The Picture of Dorian Gray:

The studio was filled with the rich odour of roses, and when
the light summer wind stirred amidst the trees of the
garden, there came through the open door the heavy scent
of the lilac, or the more delicate perfume of the pink-
flowering thorn.

From the corner of the divan of Persian saddle-bags on
which he was lying, smoking, as was his custom,
innumerable cigarettes, Lord Henry Wotton could just catch
the gleam of the honey-sweet and honey-coloured blossoms
of a laburnum, whose tremulous branches seemed hardly
able to bear the burden of a beauty so flame-like as theirs;
and now and then the fantastic shadows of birds in flight
flitted across the long tussore-silk curtains that were
stretched in front of the huge window, producing a kind of
momentary Japanese effect, and making him think of those
pallid jade-faced painters of Tokio who, through the medium
of an art that is necessarily immobile, seek to convey the
sense of swiftness and motion. The sullen murmur of the
bees shouldering their way through the long unmown grass,
or circling with monotonous insistence round the dusty gilt
horns of the straggling woodbine, seemed to make the
stillness more oppressive.

Doyle's opening is brusque, clinical, to the point; Wilde's is characteristically languorous and flowery; but the two are complementary, and both take their inspiration from drugs. Cocaine and nicotine, I can now reveal to you, are merely substitutes for Shamrock Tea, whose use was known to both authors: indeed, it inspired much of their finest work. Note especially Wilde's references to the enhanced olfactory faculty, and the illusion of motion produced by art, not to mention the presence of bees. These are symptoms you will recognize from your own experiences.

Wilde's novel is an allegory of how worldly treasure is worthless, compared to the riches of the soul; in Doyle's story, the object of the crime is a treasure-trove, and the criminals are lost souls. It will be your mission, too, should you wish to join us, to exercise your powers in search of treasure: but more of that anon. In the meantime, remember Holmes's cry to Watson at the end of the first chapter of *The Sign of Four*: *What is the use of having powers, when one has no field upon which to exert them?*

73

CINNAMON

Let me continue, said Celestine, by quoting to you another three passages: the first, from *The Sign of Four*; the second, from *The Picture of Dorian Gray*; and the third, from the journal for the year 1874 of the Jesuit priest and poet, Fr Gerard Hopkins.

There were one hundred and forty-three diamonds of the first water, including one which has been called, I believe, 'the Great Mogul', and is said to be the second largest stone in existence. Then there were ninety-seven very fine emeralds, and one hundred and seventy rubies, some of which, however, were small. There were forty carbuncles, two hundred and ten sapphires, sixty-one agates, and a great quantity of beryls, onyxes, cats'-eyes, turquoises and other stones, the very names of which I did not know at the time, though I have become more familiar with them since. Besides this, there were nearly three hundred very fine pearls, twelve of which were set in a gold coronet.

*

On one occasion he took up the study of jewels, and appeared at a costume ball as Anne de Joyeuse, Admiral of France, in a dress covered with five hundred and sixty pearls. This taste enthralled him for years, and, indeed, may be said never to have left him. He would often spend a whole day settling and resettling in their cases the various stones he had collected, such as the olive-green chrysoberyl that turns red by lamplight, the cymophane with its wire-like line of silver, the pistachio-coloured peridot, the rose-pink and wine-yellow topazes, carbuncles of fiery scarlet with tremulous four-rayed stars, flame-red cinnamon-stones, orange and violet spinels, and amethysts with their alternate layers of ruby and sapphire.

April 9 – To Kensington Museum . . . I made the following notes on gems – Beryl, watery green; carnelian, strong flesh red, Indian red; almandine, purplish red; chalcedony, some milky blue, some opalescent blue-green, some blue-green with sparkles, some dull yellow green, dull olive, lilac, white; jacinth, brownish red, dull tawny scarlet; chrysoprase, beautiful half-transparent green, some dull with dark cloudings; sardonyx, milky blue flake in brown; topaz, white, madder, sherry-colour, yellow, pale blue, wallflower red; 'dark sard' seemed purplish black; jaspar (or chalcedony) dull flesh brown; chrsyolith, bluish with yellow gleam or vice versa, also pale yellow-green, also yellow – transparent; cymophane, beautiful stone and name.

Let us further compare this fascination with gemstones with the vision of the new Jerusalem described by St John in the Book of Revelation:

And the foundations of the wall of the city were garnished with all manner of precious stones. The first foundation was jasper; the second, sapphire; the third, a chalcedony; the fourth, an emerald; the fifth, sardonyx; the sixth, sardius; the seventh, chrysolyte; the eighth, beryl; the ninth, a topaz; the tenth, a chrsysoprasus; the eleventh, a jacinth; the twelfth, an amethyst.

These are the jewels in the crown of God the Father, as depicted by Jan van Eyck in the great altarpiece at Ghent. They are symbols of the transcendental glory of the One, Holy, Catholic and Apostolic Roman Church. They are the light of the eye. They illuminate the new Jerusalem, which we will build, with your help, in Ireland's green and pleasant land. Arthur Conan Doyle was born a Catholic; Hopkins became a Catholic; Wilde died a Catholic; we are all Catholics in this together.

74

CARNATION

Celestine paused to take a handkerchief from his pocket and wipe a tear from his eye. When he had recovered his emotions, he continued: It is said of Wilde that his conversation was persuasive and astonishing, excelling in giving a certificate of truth to what was improbable. Of a fable he made a thing which had actually happened, from a thing which had actually happened he drew out a fable. Let us imagine his presence that night in London with Conan Doyle: Doyle in his sensible tweeds, Wilde wearing a cravat of greenish silk in which sparkled an amethyst tie-pin, a green carnation in his buttonhole, while his blue eyes would sometimes reflect the gold tip of his Egyptian cigarette or the green glint of his scarab ring.

Doyle has left a sketch of the meeting in his *Memories and Recollections*, published in 1924. Wilde, he recalls, had a curious precision of statement, a delicate flavour of humour, and a trick of small gestures to illustrate his meaning, which were peculiar to himself. The effect could not be reproduced, but Doyle remembers how, in discussing wars of the future, Wilde said: 'A chemist on each side will approach the frontier with a bottle' – his upraised hand and precise face conjuring up a vivid and grotesque picture.

What then followed is unpublished, but you may consult the record for yourselves in this very library, together with Doyle's manuscript of *The Coming of the Fairies*, completed in 1922, in which he postulates a universe of infinite vibrations beyond the colour spectrum which makes up the limits of our vision. In this he was correct: his mistake was not that he believed in fairies, but that he believed the two children who claimed to have photographed them.

But to return to Wilde and Doyle: when queried as to what chemicals might be deployed in future wars, Wilde, on second thoughts, saw no need for elaborate technical equipment. His own mother had a recipe – here, he pretended to be 'Speranza' for a moment, tall, pale, magnificent, and mysterious in her black lace mantilla – for an infusion of herbs, given to her by an old woman of the North, which would make anyone who drank it see the world through rose-tinted glasses, or rather green-tinted glasses, for it was called Shamrock Tea. It was a true catholicon, and most effective in banishing all thoughts of enmity, for the drinker was moved to see the world as art, and not as life, which inevitably ends in death. In the future, he declared, nations would wage peace, and not war. One had merely to infiltrate the London water supply with Speranza's cordial and the afternoon ritual of the middle classes would truly become High Tea. Ireland would then grant Home Rule to England, under the emblem of a green rose.

Doyle was spellbound, for Wilde's apparent flight of fancy was corroborated by his own experience. Two years earlier, in the autumn of 1887, while on a cycling holiday of the Mournes, he had called to Loyola House, to renew his acquaintanceship with Fr Gerard Hopkins, who was resident here at the time. They had, of course, first met at our sister college of Stonyhurst, Doyle's *alma mater*. Doyle had in his saddlebag the second draft of *A Study in Scarlet*, the first Sherlock Holmes story, which had already been rejected by two publishers, who thought the methods of its protagonist a little too implausible for the public taste. Doyle was taken to Fr Hopkins, who was reading his breviary in one of the herb gardens. It was coming up to four o'clock on a balmy September afternoon, the 18th, to be precise, the feast day of Joseph of Cupertino, the patron saint of flying; and Fr Hopkins suggested to Doyle that he join him for some tea.

75

HONEYDEW

Doyle was somewhat taken aback when Fr Hopkins led him down the garden path to what appeared to be a potting shed. Seeing his discomfiture, the Jesuit gently explained that he felt ill at ease in general company and, since coming to Loyola, preferred to take his tea with one of the under-gardeners, Br Yates. He made an excellent beverage, which reminded him very much of that brewed by Br Considine, back in the old days at Stonyhurst. Did Doyle recollect him? Yes, indeed, said Doyle, wasn't he the one that had all the stories about the Irish fairies? Fr Hopkins nodded thoughtfully.

They found Br Yates sitting on an orange-box in the shed, tending a turf stove on which a kettle was about to come to the boil. He told them that there was no tea like Shamrock Tea, and not to believe otherwise, for a cup or two of it made you see the world straight and if a man can't see the world straight he's liable to keel over. His mother back in County Sligo had drunk a couple of pots a day for eighty years, and she was straight as a rush till the day she died, and the minute she died, he said, she folded up like a jack-knife, and it took four strong men to put her in her coffin, God rest her.

It isn't many knows about the Shamrock Tea, he said, but what odds, for what's proven now was once beyond belief, and 'twas my mother got the Tea herself from a little man in a peeler's jacket that was riding a March hare one day above on Ben Bulben, for wasn't it St Patrick's day itself when she ran into him?

He gestured to them to sit down and, rummaging in the folds of his soutane, produced a yellow honeydew tobacco tin. With grave ceremony he undid the lid and sprinkled three hefty pinches of a greenish substance into a blackened teapot. A plume of steam appeared from the spout of the kettle; as he poured boiling water in, Doyle recalls, the teapot seemed to hiss with pleasure.

Don't believe all that stuff about warming the pot, said Br Yates, sure doesn't the pot get warm enough when it's on the stove. And none of your fancy milk and sugar, neither; it's the good raw bar we need.

When the tea had drawn to his satisfaction, he filled three chipped cups, and the trio began to drink. Doyle sipped gingerly at first: the taste was faintly acerbic, the scent like that of burning hay. After some minutes, he noticed the broad shaft of sunlight that beamed in through the open door of the shed, illuminating the bumps and dimples of the floor. Yes, it was truly a balmy afternoon. He followed the light into the herb garden, where it seemed to pick out every stalk, every leaf of the greenery. Late bees were bumbling about in the golden, pollen-laden air.

He causeth the grass to grow for cattle, and herb for the service of man, said Br Yates, contentedly. *For he on honeydew hath fed, and drunk the milk of Paradise.* I sometimes feel I could sit here all day with not a bother about me. But there's work to be done, and do you know, when I get to be about my work, there's not a bother about it neither. 'Tis the bee's knees. Oh, the bee's knees surely. I'll be seeing you lads later.

He wandered purposefully into the sunshine. Hopkins looked at Doyle beatifically.

Would you care for a stroll? he said.

Within half an hour, Hopkins and Doyle found themselves on the lower slopes of Slieve Commedagh, approaching the Diamond Rocks. They were in the Silent Valley, but it was far from silent: all around them, water gushed and trickled and purled, hushing through bogland, clinking over the bright pebbles of innumerable rills.

Suddenly, Hopkins stopped, stooped, and picked up a stone. He looked at it.

76

BRICK RED

Chalcedony, he whispered. Revelation 21:19. One of the foundations of the City of God. From Greek *khalkedon*, a mystical stone. Perhaps from *Khalkedon*, Chalcedon, that long-lost city of the Greeks. But surely they are the same thing. Opalescent blue-green with sparkles.

Hopkins and Doyle walked on up the slope that glittered with flashes of water and stones. Hopkins stooped again. Sardonyx, perhaps from Sardis, lost city of Asia Minor. Onyx, meaning 'nail'. Milky blue veins embedded in fingernail brown.

Then he stumbled on another, and another: topaz, also the name of a South American humming-bird; amethyst, from the Greek for drunkenness, for gazing into it was thought to be a cure; jacinth, from the youth Hyacinthus, who was turned into a blue flower by the gods.

We are princes of Serendip, you and I, he said to Doyle.

His two hands were full of precious stones. He chinked them together, and the valley responded with a series of tiny echoes rippling down across the granite outcrops until they dwindled away into silence except for the rush of the wind and the waters all around them, and the music of unseen birds.

Here, Doyle, look through the chalcedony, said Hopkins. What do you see?

Doyle remembers taking the stone from Hopkins and holding it up to his eye like a monocle. The valley shimmered before his eyes and then sprang into stereoscopic focus. He had never seen such colours before; names did not exist for such heathery blues and purples, nor the countless shades of green. Then he saw that the whole hillside was teeming and chittering with insects. Small bright birds scuttled among the dense undergrowth. Rabbits abounded from warrens. A hare ran zig-zag across his field of vision. The rock formations began to take on faces, weather-beaten, furrowed, immensely wise. Cloud-shadow raced over everything, changing it second by second, like the future being sucked into the immanence of now.

But there is a whole other world out there! he cried.

Yes, said Hopkins. *If the doors of perception were cleansed, everything would appear as it is, infinite.* But all this will soon be gone. The city of Belfast grows day by day, throwing its red-brick tentacles out into the countryside. It is building great boats. Its tobacco industry is second to none in the Empire. Its ropewalks are the longest in Europe. And for all this, they need water. Already negotiations are under way to purchase the Silent Valley and its catchment area, and to turn it into a vast reservoir. All this beauty will be drowned. We must stop them, Doyle.

*

As to what happened, or what was said next, said Celestine, we have no way of knowing. Doyle's journal for that day trails off into a meaningless scribble. After his visit to Loyola, he never saw Fr Hopkins again, but the next entry, headed London, 23 September 1887, reads as follows:

> Hopkins on bees. Recommended Proverbs 6:8, *Consider the bee and see how she labours*, and Clement of Alexandria's commentary, 'for the bee draws the nectar from a whole field of flowers to make a single drop of honey'. The Hebrew for 'bee', *dbure*, comes from the same root as that for 'word', *dbr*. The bee is an emblem of the Mormons. Revised *A Study in Scarlet* in this light . . . after drinking last of Br Yates' Tea.

A Study in Scarlet, which features the murder of two Mormons, appeared in *Beeton's Christmas Annual* for 1887, and was published in book form in 1888, the year of Hopkins's death from typhoid.

77

Silk Black

Before he consumed the last of the Tea given to him as a farewell gift by Br Yates, Doyle attempted to isolate its ingredients. He had supposed the appellation of 'shamrock' to be purely metaphorical and was therefore surprised to find traces of that herb in the mix. Upon consulting his library, he found that there was more to shamrock than meets the eye. Pliny remarks that its leaves tremble and stand up against the coming of a storm or tempest: Doyle concluded that shamrock must be sympathetic to the earth's magnetic field. Linnaeus, in his *Flora Lapponica*, bears witness to 'the swift and agile Irish, who nourish themselves with their shamrock; for they make a bread from the flowers of this plant, breathing honey odour; and the mead from shamrock honey is considered by them to bestow second sight on whomsoever drinks it'. Gerard's *Herbal* states that shamrock attracts bees more than any other common herb.

Also present in Shamrock Tea were Aconite, Belladonna and Coltsfoot, as well as elements that Doyle was unable to identify.

Experimenting with various ratios of these ingredients, he managed to concoct a mildy euphoric brew; but he could not reproduce the spectacular properties of the real thing. Nevertheless, he did not feel that his experience of Shamrock Tea had been transient, for it had permanently altered his perception of the world, of which no detail could be deemed insignificant, since the whole universe is perfused with signs. That knowledge would be with him till the day he died.

Arthur Conan Doyle died on 7 July 1930, the feast of St Boisil, whose manuscript copy of the Gospel of John, that which begins, *In the beginning was the word*, is preserved in Stonyhurst College.

As for Wilde, the story of his tragic demise is too well known to relate here. Let me merely point out a few relevant details. On 28 February 1895, Wilde received a card from the Marquis of Queensberry accusing him of indecent conduct; it was the feast day of Thomas of Aquinas, patron saint of theologians, and of pencil-makers. On 1 March, he obtained a warrant for the arrest of Queensberry on a charge of criminal libel; it was the feast of St David, patron of Wales, and of poets. On 3 April, the trial commenced; it was the feast of Irene, patron saint of peace, and of Richard de Wyse, patron saint of coachmen. On 5 April, Wilde was forced, under the cross-examination of Edward Carson, to withdraw the charge; it was the feast day of St Vincent Ferrer, whose conversion was occasioned by a false accusation of theft, and whose subsequent eloquence in the pulpit led to a rumour that bees had swarmed into his mouth when he was a baby. Wilde was arrested the same day, and on 26 April appeared at the Old Bailey on a charge of gross indecency. It was the feast of St

Anacletus, whose existence is maintained by some to be a fiction; and it was the sixth birthday of Ludwig Wittgenstein. Wilde was released on bail, and entered the dock again on 22 May, the feast of St Rita of Cascia, whose body is preserved incorrupt, and exudes an odour of roses. On 25 May he was sentenced to two years' hard labour; it was the feast of the Venerable Bede, patron saint of scholars, and of St Zenobius, whose patronage of children was confirmed by the fact that he once raised a child from the dead.

Here my uncle Celestine paused for breath.

78

POPPY

Of the many subsequent relevant dates, he continued, I will mention only three. On 19 May 1897, Wilde was released from imprisonment; it was the feast of Pope Celestine V, patron saint of bookbinders, for whom I, Celestine Carson, am named. On 8 February 1898, Wilde published *The Ballad of Reading Gaol*, a bitter denunciation of the prison system. It was the forty-fourth birthday of Edward Carson, and the feast of St Apollonia, patron of those suffering from toothache; Wilde's teeth, after two years of a prison diet, were notoriously bad. Oscar O'Flahertie Fingal Wills Wilde died in Paris on 30 November 1900, the feast of St Andrew, patron of Scotland, who was crucified on an X-shaped cross, because he would not worship false gods.

Wilde's glory, and his tragedy, was that he refused to distinguish art from life. At his trial, *The Picture of Dorian Gray* was cited as a damning piece of evidence against him. Conan Doyle thought it one of the most moral books ever written; for he and

Wilde had been imbued by the spirit of Shamrock Tea, through which we see the world as it is – infinite.

When I told people of my mother's Shamrock Tea, Wilde said to Doyle that evening in 1889, they took it for a fable; but you, my dear Doyle, are the first man I have met who knows it to be true. From now on, I will never relate it again, because it is true.

Once upon a time, continued Wilde, there was a man who was beloved in his village because he told stories. Every morning he would leave the village, and in the evening he would return, after the workmen there had done their day's work. They would gather about him and ask him, What did you see today? And he would reply, I saw a faun in a forest playing a flute, and the wild beasts danced to his music. What else did you see? said the men, and he replied, I came to the seashore, where I saw three mermaids sitting on a rock, combing their green hair with a golden comb. And the men loved him because he told stories.

One morning, he left the village, and when he came to the seashore, what did he see but three mermaids combing their green hair with a golden comb. He walked on, into the forest, where he saw a faun charming the wild beasts with the music of his flute. And when he came back to the village that evening, the men gathered about him, and asked him what he had seen.

I saw nothing, he answered.

So, my dear Doyle, of some things it is better to remain silent.

Let me finish this account of Wilde, said Celestine, with some passages from Wilde's *De Profundis*:

I said in *Dorian Gray* that the great sins of the world take place in the brain; but it is in the brain that everything takes place. We know now that we do not see with the eyes or hear with the ears. They are really channels for the transmission, adequate or inadequate, of sense impressions. It is in the brain that the poppy is red, that the apple is odorous, that the skylark sings . . .

I hope to be at least a month with my friends, and to gain peace and balance, and a less troubled heart, and a sweeter mood; and then if I feel able I shall arrange through R— to go to some quiet foreign place like Bruges, whose grey houses and green canals and cool still ways had a charm for me years ago . . .

Nature will cleanse me in great waters, and with bitter herbs make me whole.

79

WHISKEY

Our mission, said my uncle Celestine, is clear. Ireland has been too long divided. It has been said that the border between North and South exists more in the mind than in any geographical reality; we must, therefore, alter that mind-set. *Everything takes place in the brain.* When, in 1924, the Irish Border Commission met to review the arrangements set in place by the Partition Act of 1920, the only words available to the Commission were these: '. . . shall determine in accordance with the wishes of the inhabitants, so far as may be compatible with economic and geographical conditions, the boundaries between Northern Ireland and the rest of Ireland . . .'

One of the many disputed areas was South Down, where the Silent Valley Reservoir is now situated. It was clear that South Down had a substantial Catholic majority, and wished to secede to the South. Yet, by a piece of legalistic legerdemain, it was argued that 'the wishes of the inhabitants' must refer to the inhabitants of Belfast, since it was they who would most benefit from the immense body of water then being created in the Silent Valley: you will recall that the foundation sod for the dam was cut by Lord Edward Carson in the autumn of 1923; and it was Lord Edward Carson who, more than any one man, had been responsible for the very creation of the state of Northern Ireland.

Belfast would cease to be an industrial centre without the water of South Down. South Down was therefore deemed to be an integral part of Northern Ireland, as were all the other regions in which there was a Catholic majority. The border remained as it had been, a device for creating a viable economic unit which could be ruled by a Protestant majority. Without the Silent Valley, the Northern Ireland state would not exist; but, by the grace of God, the Silent Valley will be Northern Ireland's downfall.

Our plan is beautiful, and simple: we will infiltrate the water of the Silent Valley with a powerful concentration of Shamrock Tea. The inhabitants of Belfast will have Shamrock Tea in their tea, in their coffee, in their whiskey; they will wash themselves in Shamrock Tea, and be baptized with Shamrock Tea. They will see the world as it really is, a world in which everything connects; where the Many is One, and the One is Many. There will be no division, for everything in the real world refers to something else, which leads to something else again, in a never-ending hymn of praise. The world is an eternal story.

We have laboured for decades for this moment. All it requires now is your co-operation; for sufficient quantities of Tea are not, at this moment in time, available to us. The Tea you were given belongs to a dwindling stock, passed down throughout the centuries; it is believed that the old woman of the North who gave

Lady Wilde her supply was the last person on earth to know the recipe, which then died with her.

This is not an insurmountable difficulty. You two boys – you, Maeterlinck, and you, my nephew, for though you are not my real nephew, I think of you as one – have been trained since infancy for this task, as has my 'daughter', Berenice. In a few moments she will join you. I will then leave you alone, for you three alone must discuss this momentous issue, and make your own decision on it; for without free will, there can be no freedom. Without free will there can be no future, for the future will be rooted to the past.

To all intents and purposes, Shamrock Tea is now a thing of the past, and exists only in the past. You must therefore go back into the past in order to retrieve the future. Goodbye for now. I will call again on you in three hours.

Celestine bowed formally and left the room walking backwards, as if reluctant to let us out of his sight for more time than was necessary. With that, Berenice appeared.

80

SAFFRON

She was dressed in her St Dympna's uniform: white blouse, shamrock green and saffron striped tie, white blouse, white knee-socks, black wedge-soled shoes, grass-green skirt and matching jacket, whose pocket was badged with an image of Dympna holding the chain of a bound demon. I thought it became her well. I saw again how green her eyes were, how raven-black her hair. I kissed her on both cheeks and introduced her to Maeterlinck, who did likewise, in a very Belgian fashion.

I'm pleased to meet you, said Berenice. I have heard much about you. In fact, I have read a book about you: the Blue Book, is it not? I also read a book about dear coz here, the Yellow Book. I am the Green Book. So we three books together make up a little colour library, whose volumes we can interchange at will. We can make many different colours of a spectrum. We can defy gravity; at times, we defy time. When we remember our past, it stands vividly before us, in full colour. We inhale the odours of the past.

I know this because I know more than you. I know it because

Mother Superior used to stand me in front of the Picture for an hour every day. You know, the van Eyck picture of the man and wife, where you and I have been before, coz. And I know that they mean us to go into the Picture, for there is a treasure in the Picture which they greatly desire, for they say it will make all men and women free. That treasure must be Shamrock Tea. In what shape or form it exists, I do not know. But it could lie in the crown of the man's hat, or the lady's plaits, or in the wire-haired dog. It could be in the chandelier, or the flame of the candle that burns in it. It could very well be the mirror, or in the mirror. It could be the carved lion, or the gargoyle with two backs. But they mean us to get it.

The question is, said Berenice dramatically, should we?

Let me put it this way: we three have been singled out, it would appear, since babes-in-arms, or rather not-in-arms because as far as I can work out they snatched us from our cradles, like the fairies do, and brought us up in their fairy ways. We wore the clothes they gave to us, we ate the food they specially prepared for us, we drank the drinks they made up. The drinks especially. Since we were the age of four they spiked our drinks with Shamrock Tea; you remember the days when you saw things you'd never seen before. Is it any wonder we are the way we are?

I am grateful for parts of it. How could I not be, for how could I otherwise be? I must be who I am. I love the clarity of the world because of it. You know, the way things gleam at you, it might be a china cup, or a primrose in a hedge, or a dented aluminium wash-basin, and they seem to share with you their contentment at being just what they are. I speak a language like no others except you. You are my brothers, and I am your sister; and I must look after you. We are the only family we have. We are the Silent Three, who glide around the corridors when everyone else is in bed. Three is Christ between two thieves. We are the three leaves of the trefoil. We three are Shamrock Tea.

81

RED HEN

Yet how can I be sure of anything? continued Berenice. When I stood in front of the Picture, sometimes I thought I knew: for that was a world I had got to know and love. I loved the deep vermilion of the curtains, I loved the wire-haired dog, I loved the Turkish rug. I loved the lady's little red pattens, and the palpable grain in the man's bare wooden clogs. I could feel the amber rosary beads between my fingers. I breathed the perfume of the oranges and the smell of burning wax. Then I'd blink and it would all be gone, and I was standing outside the Picture again. Sleet fell across the darkening countryside beyond the study window and I was back in what they call the Real World.

So, before we proceed, before I know entirely what is going on, and whether we go along with it or not, you must give me your accounts. You, Maeterlinck, will you go first?

I scarcely know what to think, said Maeterlinck. If we pursue Celestine's analogy of the bees, then we have been living our lives in a glass hive: can we presume our observers are benevo-lent? Then again, perhaps we are the Three Princes of Serendip, or rather, two princes and a princess, who have the gift of making discoveries of things we are not in quest of. I am reminded that Serendip is an ancient name for Ceylon, and that some of the postage stamps of that British colony bore an image of the coconut palm, whose seeds are dispersed by ocean currents. Perhaps we are like coconuts, thus brought fortuitously together, making a little grove of three.

The study of stamps gives us insights into the wider world. The coconut appears under the crowned head of George VI: we thus know that there were five King Georges before him, and we learn with interest that the Third was mad. The coconut itself is an emblem of the vast wealth of the Empire on whose stamps it appears: for every part of the coconut affords profit to man, not least its oil. The rough fibres of the nuts are used for stuffing mattresses, and for making matting; sugar and alcohol are made from the bud of the palm; the wood, too, is valuable; the shells make excellent fuel; and the roots provide a narcotic drug. Perhaps the coconut is a form of Shamrock Tea: but it is carefully controlled by the imperial managers, who allow the natives their nirvana so as to enslave them. Are we, then, like them?

To be or not to be, that is the question; whether to cross the fron-tier our guardians have postulated for us, or to draw a frontier about ourselves, behind which we maintain our private realm — *the undiscovered country from whose bourn no traveller returns*. Yet I have an urge to see the country in the van Eyck painting. When I lived in Ghent, nothing was so pleasurable as to get lost in its labyrinth of alleyways and streets, little entries leading into high courtyards, or walled orchards, or a stone-flagged backyard with whitewashed outhouses, and red hens pecking at the yellow sand.

I would like to go back to the Bruges of van Eyck.

82

PAWNBROKER'S GOLD

Even though my childhood had been spent exploring Ghent, I grew to realize it was unfathomable, and that the permutations of streets one could walk in order to arrive at any given destination bordered on infinity. Moreover, the experience of entering any given street from one given street instead of another would be completely different. Thus, entering Rue des Chanterelles from Rue de la Cuiller, one was aware of the little café on one corner of the intersection, the *boulangerie* on the other; whereas, emerging from Rue Guillaume Tell, one would immediately see the guns and tackle shop directly opposite, hemmed in by a dress designer's and a signboard painter's.

The signs themselves fascinated me: the giant scissors cutting the air outside a tailor's; the revolving red and white stripes of a barber's pole, signifying a bandage wound around an arm prior to its being let of blood; the pawnbroker's three golden balls, emblem of the merchant bankers the Medicis, and of St Nicholas of Bari, who gave three purses of gold to three virgin sisters to enable them to marry. Every trade bespoke itself; and the street names were eloquent of former designations, some of which still lingered powerfully, as in the warm smell of bread baking in Rue des Baguettes, or the wind whispering through the leaves of the single aspen in Rue Tremble.

On feast days the tall, leaning houses were hung with banners: some a rich dark blue with a yellow star in the centre; others all black with a narrow border of blue and yellow, enclosing the Golden Lion of Flanders; these intermingled with the Belgian national colours of red, yellow and black vertical stripes. Drums and bugles sounded; trams clanged their bells; dogs barked; companies of cheering soldiers tramped the streets; peasant girls linked arm-in-arm clattered along in clogs; the raucous cries of hucksters filled the air. Come dusk, the Place d'Armes was thronged. Teams of men on ladders lighted the thousands of small oil lamps strung between the trees and the bandstands, glowing like multicoloured jewels in their cups of blue, yellow, white, green and red glass. My dreams during those nights resounded to the clash of brass and the deep boom of drums, the clapping of hands, the cheering and the singing of folk songs. It was dawn before the band concluded the festivities with the playing of the Belgian anthem, emptying the streets and squares.

As the chimes from the belfry heralded the new day, my heart would fill with a deep affection for our nation. And yet, at that time, the street names were in French; now they are in Flemish. This leads me to consider that our country, too, has long been divided, and has languished in the toils of internecine language-war for centuries. Many Belgians are bilingual: van Eyck spoke both Flemish, the language of the street and the workshop, and French, the language of the court which employed him. But the majority are monoglot; knowing only their father or their mother tongue, they are deprived of knowing how the other half lives. Sometimes in my dreams there is only one language, and there are no frontiers between one being and another.

Perhaps a dose of Shamrock Tea would do the Belgians no harm. If we take your guardian Celestine at his word, and we have no reason to disbelieve him, he too was once like one of us. He knew his visions to be realities. So I am inclined to go along with his plan, Maeterlinck concluded.

83

AMBER

Yes, replied Berenice, you could say that my guardian has been a bit of a peeping Tom with regard to me and my cousin, examining us in our glass hive; but at least he has made a clean breast of it and seems to have laid most of his cards on the table, unlike some I could name. I mean, you would not believe the nuns at St Dympna's, going around rattling their rosary beads at you. For all their talk of the next world, their eyes were fixed on the empty forms of this one: the cut of a school blazer, or the height of a skirt's hemline, or whether the top button of a shirt was left undone or not. Religiously, they would stand me in front of the Picture every day; and I knew that they saw nothing. For them it was only a painting, colours brushed on to a board, not a door to another world.

But you, my cousin, she said, turning to me, what are your conclusions?

Hearing Maeterlinck speak of Ghent, I said, I was reminded of

Belfast. Like him, I used to spend hours exploring my native city. The Smithfield quarter I found particularly intriguing, a veritable rookery of hallways, alleyways and gangways leading up to balconies – each with its nest of dwelling places – higher and ever higher, while the lower levels rang to the noise of all kinds of trades: coopers, wheelwrights, coffin-makers, blacksmiths. Here, too, bowed over their lathes in dusty ateliers, were the musical instrument-makers and the wood-carvers. Some of their products found an outlet in the vast covered market, whose labyrinth of glass-roofed aisles and arcades, swarming with a buzzing multitude of buyers, dealers and idle passers-by, seemed emblematic of the city as a whole.

But this was mainly the empire of the second-hand. Its stalls and booths were crammed like Aladdin's caves with bric-à-brac: old china, watches, jewellery, furniture, paintings, books; boxes of old light-fittings and spark-plugs, buttons, coins, glass marbles, spectacles, worn briar pipes and bitten cigarette-holders, scent-bottles, bunches of ancient keys. I often wondered about their former lives. Sometimes, handling a carved ivory figurine, or running a string of amber beads through my fingers, I would get a palpable shock: a brightly coloured scene would flash into my inward eye and I knew I breathed the perfume of another space and time.

Snatches of hushed talk and seditious verses wafted from the open doors of public houses down narrow streets smelling of rum and tobacco. The eighteenth century was just a turn around the corner, where everything seemed possible. Revolution was at hand; Catholics joined Protestants in preaching treason, *liberté*, *égalité, fraternité*. Napoleon was a rising star. Minute by minute, the future was invented; new colours, as predicted by clairvoyants, appeared in the spectrum, for the world was spun from infinite vibrations of the ether. Hitherto covert shades of green – oak-leaf, laurel, emerald – became all the rage; gentlemen of fashion peered through green beryl quizzing-glasses. The ancient harp of Ireland was revived, and appeared embroidered in gold thread on green banners.

Only a thin veil shimmered between this world and that. Sometimes, it would blow away like gunsmoke, and I could see the past as clear as now. Then it would fade, as did that dream of freedom. If Shamrock Tea empowers us to bring that possibility within reach again, it is then, I think, our duty to embrace it. I say we go into the Picture.

We are all agreed, then? said Berenice.

We are, said Maeterlinck and I.

All for one, and one for all, said Berenice.

84

UNIFORM GREEN

So we became the Silent Three I'd read about in Berenice's school stories. Soon after our conference, Celestine appeared. Over his tweed suit he wore a cape, or cope, of fine green wool, embroidered with harps, shamrocks and crosses; in his right hand, he carried an oak staff with a bronze serpent coiled around it. He looked at us like a kindly bishop.

You have decided?

We have, said Berenice.

The verdict?

We will do whatever needs to be done, she answered firmly.

I am overjoyed, said Celestine. And now, we must move quickly, for much remains to be told before you embark on your historic mission. Come with me.

Staff in hand, Celestine led us through the library. By now, the November light had almost failed, but shafts of weak sunshine still penetrated the trefoil windows of the western colonnade, throwing a dim glow on the gold-blocked spines of the books; and I thought again of the wealth of knowledge contained therein, a world of facts beyond the grasp of any one person. Yet each had contributed their solitary labours to that vast community, and I felt a tremor of excitement at the part that we three were to play in rewriting the history book of Ireland.

Through long corridors and up winding stairs we travelled, till we arrived at Fr Brown's study. Celestine knocked formally three times with his staff. The door opened. Standing before us was a man dressed similarly to Celestine. I heard Maeterlinck gasp. I looked at him; he had grown pale. Allow me, he whispered, to introduce you to my uncle Maurice.

I am deeply sorry, said Maeterlinck's uncle Maurice to Maeterlinck, for appearing so suddenly to you, but I felt I could not meet you before, lest I influence your decision. Remember, sometimes the bees swarm when least expected. Free will, you understand. You will forgive me, I hope.

Of course, said Maeterlinck. How could it be otherwise?

We entered the room. Since our last interview with the Director-General, it appeared to have increased in size, for it now accommodated a long oak refectory table, around which, besides Fr Brown, seven men were seated, each dressed in uniform green copes. On the table were two tall tea urns of chased silver, one of which had three spouts. There were twelve Belleek china shamrock pattern tea-cups and saucers, and three clay pipes stamped with a harp and shamrock motif. Above the mantel hung the van Eyck Double Portrait. Never had it seemed more alluring, as its gem-like colours flickered above the shifting flames of the fire.

Sit down, sit down, said Fr Brown warmly. Let me welcome you to this, the most important Tea Party in the history of the Third Chapter of the Ancient Order of Hibernians, as constituted by we nine men. I need not make introductions. Names are not important, for we are all as one in this regard. Brother Celestine will have already outlined to you some of our *raisons d'être*. My role is to brief you on the mechanics of your mission. You will have already guessed that you must enter the Picture; in order to do so successfully, you must know something of its history.

Berenice, Maeterlinck and I sat down, and Fr Brown began the story of the Arnolfini Double Portrait.

85

BURGUNDY

First of all, said Fr Brown, the painting that you see before you is not a reproduction, as the term is usually understood, of the Arnolfini Double Portrait. The painting of that name which hangs in the National Gallery in London is not a copy of this one; yet both are authentic van Eycks. This is not a paradox. It was standard practice for the workshops of fifteenth-century Flanders to create multiple versions of well-known paintings: some were made by acknowledged masters, of their own works; some were assigned to apprentices; and some were a combination of both, so that even a square centimetre of painting could be the work of several hands.

The archive of the Collège de Sainte-Barbe in Ghent holds a notarized copy of the will of Anselmo Adornes of Bruges, made in 1470, which bequeaths to each of his three daughters 'a panel wherein there is a St Francis depicted by the hand of Jan van Eyck'. Whether this refers to the St Francis alone, or to the whole panel, is unclear, for the three panels have since been lost.

Also lost are all the works made by van Eyck at the command of his chief employer, Philip the Good, Duke of Burgundy.

Jan van Eyck was appointed *valet de chambre* to Philip the Good on 19 May 1425; appropriately, it was the feast of Celestine V, patron saint of bookbinders, for whom our good brother here is named. Let us recall the Books of Hours made by Flemish artists under the aegis of the Dukes of Burgundy, beautifully illuminated with gem-like colours, lapis lazuli, carmine, green malachite and gold: each page a miniature painting, each an emblem of a point in universal time, as represented by the Zodiac, the seasons, and the canonical hours of matins, lauds, prime, vespers and compline; hours that we in the Society of Jesus still observe. Reading such books, one paid homage to the beauty of the world, as authorized and overseen by God: for the book was a picture of the world. No expense was spared, for the Burgundian capital of Bruges was one of the richest places in the world.

There were 'oranges and lemons from Castille', says a traveller's account, 'which seemed only just to have been gathered from the trees, fruits and wine from Greece, confections and spices from Alexandria and all the Levant, just as if one were there; here was Italy with its brocades, silks and armour; Turkish and Armenian carpets were on sale in the cloisters of St Donatian'.

The sumptuousness of the Burgundian court was singularly epitomized by Philip the Good's wedding to Isabella of Portugal in 1430. After the state entry into Bruges on Sunday, 8 January — the feast of the hermit saint, Stephen of Muret, who was noted for wearing a metal breastplate instead of a hairshirt – a magnificent banquet was held. For this occasion the whole city was painted red; Venetian scarlet banners hung from the balconies. Teams of unicorns carrying leopards on their backs appeared pulling floats which bore giant pastries, from which emerged live bears, apes, parrots, four sheep whose fleece had been dyed blue, three musical monkeys, two piping goats, and a singing wolf. Men who were half griffins and half men rode on wild boars, juggling daggers and swords. Amidst a fanfare of trumpets, four giants dragged in an enormous whale, which spewed forth dancing boys and singing maidens; they quarrelled with the giants, who drove them back into the belly of Leviathan. A dragon breathing fire flew through the hall and disappeared again as mysteriously as it had come.

The fountains of the palace flowed with Burgundy wine; and, as the day wore on, many of the guests found it increasingly difficult to tell whether what they saw was make-believe, or real, or some amalgam of the two.

86

SEASICK GREEN

For his part, van Eyck presented the Duke with a Book of Hours which had *trompe l'œil* flowers strewn on the margins of the pages, with a dragonfly perched momentarily on them, painted so delicately that the flowers could be seen through its wings. But his role in the wedding of Philip the Good and the Infanta Isabella of Portugal extended much beyond that, for in 1428 the Duke had requested him to accompany a delegation to Lisbon to nego-tiate the marriage. Van Eyck's commission was to paint her portrait: not once, but twice, for the Duke had never seen the Infanta, and wanted more than a verbal guarantee of her appear-ance before he committed himself to the union.

On 16 October, the feast of St Gall, patron of birds, the ambassadors set out for the port of Sluis, from which they departed on two Venetian galleys. They landed at the English port of Sandwich, where they rested before departing for Lisbon on 13 November, the feast of Homobonus, patron saint of tailors. They were driven by gales into other English ports: Camber,

Plymouth and Falmouth, where they arrived on 25 November, the feast of Catherine of Alexandria, the patron saint of libraries. On 2 December, the feast of St Bibiana, who is invoked against hangovers, they sailed south through the Bay of Biscay and arrived at Bayonne on 11 December, the feast of Daniel the Stylite, who spent thirty-three years perched on a series of ever higher columns. They left on the fourteenth of the month, the feast of St Fortunatas, whose name speaks for itself. Finally, on 18 December, they reached Lisbon. It was the feast of St Samthann, the Irish nun who, when a monk told her he was going on pilgrimage, answered that the kingdom of heaven can be reached without crossing the sea, for God is near to all who call on Him.

They did not see the King of Portugal until 13 January 1429, the feast of Hilary of Poitiers, the patron saint of lawyers, and of those stricken by snakebite. After many days of intensive negotiations with the king's intermediaries, a provisional contract was drawn up, while enquiries were pursued as to the reputation, health and bearing of the Infanta. Meanwhile, van Eyck worked on the two portraits, which he completed by 12 February, the feast of Julian the Hospitaller, the patron saint of circus performers. The paintings were dispatched post-haste to Burgundy the next day, the feast of St Modomnoc, who was responsible for introducing apiculture to Ireland: according to the Martyrology of Oegus the Culdee, Modomnoc studied under St David in Wales, where he also tended his bees; and when the time came for Modomnoc to leave, a swarm of bees settled on his ship and accompanied him back home.

What, then, were van Eyck's portraits of Isabella of Portugal like? Were they copies of each other, or did they represent two aspects of the same face? Alas, we have no way of knowing, for they are lost. In fact, it is generally agreed that most of van Eyck's *œuvre* has been lost. However, some verbal records remain. Bartolomeo Fazio, writing in 1454, praises van Eyck's *Map of the World*, in which all the places and regions of the earth were represented in recognizable form and at measurable distances. Even more impressive was his *Women of Noble Form Emerging from a Warm Bath*, once in the possession of Cardinal Ottaviano, in which the subjects were veiled with linen drapery and steam. In the same picture a candle was shown as if it were really burning; also an old woman perspiring, and a dog lapping water. In an extensive landscape seen through the window were tiny horses and men, groves, villages and castles, elaborated with such artistry that one thing appeared to be separated from another by about fifty miles.

Nothing in this picture was more wonderful than the mirror, in which every detail was reflected as accurately as in a real mirror.

87

PYRENEAN BLUE

As you can see, continued Fr Brown, we are now beginning to approach the Arnolfini Double Portrait, and its fascinating mirror. But before we look deeper into it, let us return to van Eyck in 1429. While they awaited the Duke of Burgundy's response to the two portraits of Isabella of Portugal, the delegation decided to make a pilgrimage to Santiago de Compostela, whose shrine to St James the Great is next only to Jerusalem and Rome in the hierarchy of the holy places of Christendom.

Now, there are several parallels between St James and St Donard, who gives his name to Slieve Donard, the highest peak of the Mournes, in whose lee Loyola House is situated. Both are patrons of fishermen: James, because he was a fisherman, and Donard, because it is believed that Donard's Well, on the summit of the mountain, is connected, by a subterranean passage, to the Irish Sea. Both share 25 July as their feast day and the scallop as their emblem. It is thought that water from Donard's Well is more efficacious if drunk from a scallop shell.

Everything is connected, *sub specie aeternitatis*. If you stare into the depths of Donard's Well in broad daylight, you will see stars reflected there; and the tomb of St James in Compostela was discovered in the year 813 when a green star was seen to hover over the spot. Hence Compostela means 'the field of the star'. In the beginning, says St Augustine, God spoke the Word, and thus created heaven and earth. All things exist in that Word, which is the Book of Nature, and the Book of Revelation tells us that *the heavens shall be folded up like a scroll*. So in the eyes of God, time and space can be folded up, and things which appear to us to be centuries or miles apart are, in reality, but a parchment thickness away. If we were bookworms, we could eat into those spaces in next to no time. We are not worms, but we can, by way of Shamrock Tea, travel through those wormholes.

Van Eyck's masterpiece, *The Adoration of the Immaculate Lamb* in St Bavon's in Ghent, is perhaps as close to an eternal vision as we get on earth. In its central panel, an unearthly light shines equally on everything, from the towers of the distant city and the blue summits of the further mountains to the microscopically depicted plants in the foreground. Many commentators have ascribed some of the latter to van Eyck's sojourn in Portugal and Spain, for they include species not native to Flanders. The truth is more complicated, however; under the orange trees, the lemons and the pomegranates, among the watercress and cuckoo flowers, are herbs that we now know to form some of the chief ingredients of Shamrock Tea: to whit, Elecampane, St John's Wort, Yarrow, Aconite and Coltsfoot, to name some. Less easy to distinguish against the emerald grass, but present in abundance, are clumps of Shamrock. In the triptych above this landscape are the three central figures of the Virgin, God the Father and John the Baptist. The Virgin is reading a book which rests on a green coverlet; God wears a green stole; and John is swathed in a voluminous green cloak.

Looking for further greens, and there are many, our eye is drawn to the landscape again, where groups of apostles, prophets, saints and martyrs, popes and bishops are assembled in ritual splendour. Among the bishops is one whose face is almost concealed: all we see is the lid of his left eye, and the eyebrow of the right. But we can identify him, all the same, for he alone wears a mitre of deep green. He is St Patrick.

88

CLARET

You will not be entirely surprised when I say that van Eyck met St Patrick in person. I have said that the universe can be rolled up like a chart, or folded over on itself: indeed, we can imagine it fitting into a nutshell, like one of those Bibles written in letters illegible to the naked eye. For all we know, God might carry the universe around in His pocket like a watch. The beauty of this device is that any point in time and space can be made to correspond to any other.

To make the leap from one point to another is not easy, though sometimes we manage it in our dreams. In the waking world, certain conditions must be fulfilled. It has long been recognized that icons and other holy images are portals to the trans-temporal world. Incense is a great help. So is the monotonous chanting of prayers, and dim organ music. It is efficacious to choose an appropriate saint's feast day for one's jumping-off point. Then there is Shamrock Tea. You know from your reading that van Eyck spent some time in the Flemish town of Gheel, where, under the aegis of St Dympna, he formulated the varnish which no one has ever been able to emulate since. The reason is simple: the recipe, besides its terebinthine base, incorporated a decoction of Shamrock Tea; hence the hallucinatory clarity of his painting.

The journey from Lisbon to northern Spain in 1429 was long and arduous. It was mid-March by the time the Burgundian ambassadors reached Compostela. There, on the 17th, van Eyck visited the shrine of St James. It was not only St Patrick's Day but also that of St Gertrude of Nivelles in Belgium, who was assured by the Irish missionary, St Foillan, of the protection of St Patrick on the day of her death. Gertrude is invoked against rats and mice; she is therefore the patron saint of cats. Her emblem is a staff with a mouse running up it. St Patrick is usually portrayed with a shamrock in one hand and his staff in the other, by which means he is banishing the snakes who writhe in the foreground. Patrick and Gertrude: a powerful conjunction.

Van Eyck prepared himself for his visitation by taking a dose of Tea and by praying to both saints. The sun had just gone down and Compostela was bathed in a pale green twilight. The bells of Santiago rang out loud and clear, echoing against the red city wall and the blue wall of the mountains. Within the great cathedral, the great five-foot silver censer began to move, attached to ropes under the central dome, and swung by four men dressed in claret robes. A long swathe of incense billowed down the nave. In his dim shrine above the high altar, St James glimmered in the light of a thousand constellated tapers. Then the choir began to sing with that deep-throated bass noise heard only in Spain, and it seemed the columns of the cathedral vibrated with them. As van Eyck gazed at St James, the statue moved its head, then beckoned. He rose from where he knelt on the cold stone floor and looked up. The roof of the cathedral was gone, and in its place were stars, millions of stars, swarming like bees. As he tried to comprehend their multitudes, one star detached itself from the swarm and began to drop towards him.

Faster and faster it neared him, like a rose blossoming into his field of vision, until, opening wide its huge petals, it finally surrounded him and he was swallowed in its incandescent blaze.

89

OAK

When he came to, he found himself lying under an oak tree. A man dressed in a sheepskin was standing over him, peering into his face. He spoke unintelligible words to van Eyck, then he frowned and began again in Latin. It was an odd Latin, inflected with a guttural burr, the stresses misplaced, but van Eyck could just about make out the gist of it.

You have come a long way, said the man in the sheepskin.

I have, said van Eyck. Where am I?

You are in Hibernia. The Romans call it that because they think it is always winter here; but as you can see, it is the beginning of spring. The man stooped to the ground and plucked a green sprig from it. This is what we call shamrock, he said, and they call me Patrick. I have used this illustration before and I hope you are not too familiar with it. But you will see that it has three leaves on one stalk. These represent the past, the present and the future, which form what we call the Trinity. This means that one person can be three: the person in his memory, the person who he thinks himself to be, and the person he wishes to be. I believe this to be the truth, and I wish others to believe. Are you with me?

I am, said van Eyck, where else would I be?

I mean, do you want to be with me? To believe what we believe?

If you believe what you have just said, said van Eyck, using the second person plural, then I believe you too. I must be with you.

Then there is a little ceremony to be performed, which requires water, of which I have none at the moment, but that can soon be remedied, said St Patrick. He struck the ground with his staff, and a spring of clear water welled up from it.

What is your name? he asked van Eyck.

John, he answered.

Patrick then spoke that name, baptizing van Eyck. Van Eyck felt the cold water spill into his fontanelle like a shaft of light that went straight to his brain and opened it up. Purple mountains swayed around him. The sun danced in the blue windswept sky. Momentarily, he saw the past, the present and the future. Then he knew no more.

When he came to for the second time, he was back in Compostela, in the cathedral of Santiago, lying alone on the silent floor, his body illuminated in fits and starts by guttering candles.

Fr Brown paused. That was one of the most important moments in our history, he said. From then on, van Eyck was a changed man; and so, we have all been changed by him, by how he saw the world.

Van Eyck returned to Flanders, arriving there on Christmas

Day, 1429. On 15 January 1430, Philip the Good's wedding festivities concluded by his proclaiming the Order of the Knights of the Golden Fleece. It was the feast day of Paul the Hermit, patron saint of weavers, and of the Irish nun St Ita, known for her devotion to the Holy Trinity. The Irish connection was important, for the Knights of the Golden Fleece were none other than a branch of the Ancient Order of Hibernians. Among those made Knights that day were van Eyck himself, and Giovanni Arnolfini, an Italian merchant long resident in Bruges.

90

DRAGON GREEN

No society now existing among mankind has a more splendid and authentic lineage than the Ancient Order of Hibernians. The Freemasons lay a vague and shadowy claim to origin among those who built the tower of Babel, the Pyramids and Solomon's Temple; the Knights Templar trace a mystical descent from the Crusaders; and there are numerous societies which claim to have been founded during the Dark and Middle Ages. All these claims are unsupported by historical evidence, and arise entirely from a desire to shroud the comparatively modern origin of these societies with the mantle of antiquity.

The annals of the Ancient Order of Hibernians are a part of the history of Ireland from 1331 BC, authentically established by the most eminent authorities; and the precious sentiment of brotherhood has been a quenchless fire on the altars of that Order since Munemon, monarch of all Ireland, founded the Order of the Golden Chain. On the dark landscape of Irish history there is always visible the serried spears of the Ancient Order of

Hibernians, gleaming in the van of the human tide of patriotism. Fingal, Cuchullain, Ossian, Conn of the Hundred Battles, Niall of the Nine Hostages: all were members of that illustrious Order; among its saints were Colmcille, Brigid, Ciaran and Brendan; and the first of these was St Patrick himself.

The mention by Irish annalists of the Knights of the Golden Chain is the earliest account of chivalric orders in the history of any nation. It was the Irish who exported these notions to Gaul, and later to the region corresponding to present-day Flanders. Tacitus, Strabo and Livy, observant Roman writers, mention the torc and chains of gold used in civil and military ceremonies, and the saffron-dyed robes, exactly conforming to the description given by Irish writers. Still another proof that this order of knighthood was the first instituted in the world is the fact that they used chariots drawn by horses centuries before their use by the Romans.

Philip the Good endowed his Knights with golden chains, from which hung golden rams, signifying the Golden Fleece sought by the Argonauts, and the wealth of Flanders, which was built on its wool trade. You will recall that the Fleece of antiquity was hung on an oak tree: *Eyck* means 'oak', so van Eyck's being made a Knight of the Golden Fleece was linguistically inevitable. Jan van Eyck is a kind of John the Baptist, whose emblem is a lamb, as celebrated in van Eyck's masterpiece, *The Adoration of the Immaculate Lamb*.

Furthermore, the Golden Fleece was guarded by a dragon, which Jason overcame by a herbal potion concocted for him by Medea; among its ingredients was aconite, which also features in

Shamrock Tea. Ovid, in his account of this episode, says that Medea, drawn in her car by a team of winged dragons, spent nine days and nine nights 'traversing all lands' to gather the deadly herbs; we may be sure Ireland was included in her travels. I need not draw out these parallels any further.

Fr Brown now pointed to the Arnolfini Double Portrait.

Observe the green-tasselled string of amber beads hanging on the wall. To be sure, these form a rosary. They are also an emblem of that golden chain which links the history of Ireland and Flanders, whose beads are centuries. We are now in a position to interpret the picture in that light.

91

ORANGE TEA

The panel on which the picture is painted is made up of three Irish oak boards.

Inscribed on the back wall are the words, *Johannes de eyck fuit hic*, and the year, 1434. Add these digits and they make twelve, which is three times four. Four stands for the fourth dimension, time.

Johannes de eyck fuit hic can mean three things: 'Jan van Eyck has been here', 'Jan van Eyck has been this person', and 'Jan van Eyck has been this', that is, the oak panel of the painting, or the painting itself.

Discounting the pair reflected in the mirror, there are three figures in the painting: the man, the woman, and the dog.

The wiry dog is not reflected in the mirror. But if we imagine him turned about face, we can see his body resembles a map of Ireland, made up of infinitely complicated strands.

The man is Arnolfini, also known in French as Arnoul le Fin; that is, Arnoul the Shrewd. He is a merchant, an interpreter, a dealer in fabrics, as witnessed by his luxurious robe, an uninterrupted fall of ever-deepening folds. As painted by van Eyck, he might well be van Eyck himself.

Even more suggestive of the folds of space and time is the woman's green dress. Look at the fur-edged slit of the enormous sleeve, whose curve is decorated with vertical strips of dagging cut, like four-leaved shamrocks, into Maltese crosses; just under the gathering of the sleeve into its slit, the strips have been placed in three overlapping layers, each three crosses wide, echoing the bunching of the sleeve. Everything – folds, frills, and slashes – is looped in triplicate.

Her five layers of veils are in fact but one veil, folded backwards and forwards on itself five times. These five fifths are the five provinces of Ireland. She, too, is a map of Ireland. She is also St Dympna, patron of sleepwalkers, and of those who see visions.

The mirror's frame is toothed like the cog-wheel of a clock. The two figures in its looking-glass are about to enter the pictured room from another time and space. They are anyone and anybody. They could be me and you.

The window has six shutters, the chandelier six branches.

One lighted candle burns in one of the sconces.

One orange rests on the window-sill.

Three oranges rest on the oak chest by the window.

If we add up all these factors, said Fr Brown, the message is clear: the Double Portrait is a two-way portal. The picture now in the National Gallery, London, was made first, and by means of it van Eyck travelled to Ireland, where he made the picture which now confronts you. So the Knights of the Golden Fleece and those of the Golden Chain – the Hibernians – were amalgamated. The London picture, out of touch with its original location for centuries, exposed to the gaze of millions of unbelievers, has long since lost its power. Only our picture remains true to van Eyck's vision.

A memorandum written by van Eyck resides in our archive, telling how he painted the pictures. There then follows an account of his experience in Gheel. As a postscript, he adds that the three oranges on the oak chest have been injected with a concentrate of Shamrock Tea sufficient to affect the population of Bruges and its hinterland three times over. This, as it turns out, is a close estimation of the present-day population of the six counties of Northern Ireland.

All that remains is for you to enter the painting, contact van Eyck, and come back with the oranges. But before you go, are there any questions?

92

MADDER

I put up my hand. All the time Fr Brown had been speaking, I had felt a vague unease, which now clarified itself.

Am I right, I said, in assuming we will be travelling to fifteenth-century Bruges?

That is correct, said Fr Brown, though at what precise point in the space–time continuum, we cannot be entirely sure. But we can reasonably assume that the painting itself will provide a focus, and that you will emerge in van Eyck's studio around the time he completed the London painting, on St Luke's Day, 1434.

Forgive me for asking, I said, but when Berenice and I first entered the painting, we found ourselves in what looked like present-day County Down; and besides, we seemed to lose control of our trip. How do we know that the same thing will not happen again?

That is a fair question, replied Fr Brown, which I could answer at some length, citing the relatively low strength of Shamrock Tea you consumed that night, your inexperience of the painting's history, the fact that the painting was not in its original location, here in County Down, but in your uncle Celestine's study, and so on. When you entered the painting, did you feel yourselves to be dressed like the male and female figures?

We did, I said.

That was only to be expected, given that you were wearing mid-twentieth-century clothing. The aconite in Shamrock Tea — also known as monkshood — is a powerful corrective to perceived anachronism. You initially thought you were in 1434, hence you mentally clothed yourselves appropriately. But when you realized you were, in fact, in 1959, or thereabouts, things began to go awry, is that not so?

True, I admitted.

Now, said Fr Brown, our tailors have prepared costumes for each of you, authentic in every pleat, gusset, seam, pucker and tuck. The materials are hand-woven, hand-stitched with thread spun on a treadle spinning-wheel, dyed with natural dyes, and the whole garment sprayed with a solution of shamrock which contains a triple dose of aconite. I think you will find them satisfactory. The very dogs in the street will defer to you as citizens of fifteenth-century Bruges. Much more important for your venture is Maeterlinck, the third element. You and Berenice alone would be lost in the Bruges of 1434, even if you managed to get there, which, without Maeterlinck, is not one hundred per cent certain, for three is the magic number. Maeterlinck has breathed the air of Flanders, and he speaks its languages. Admittedly, French and Flemish have evolved somewhat since then, but he will find them comprehensible, and any difference in his pronunciation and vocabulary will be readily explained by his pretending to be the son of a Dutch merchant, accompanying his friends from Ireland, which country then, as now, enjoyed excellent relations with Flanders.

We have thought it less conspicuous to dress Berenice as a boy, since a young lady of her class would not be seen unchaperoned. Here is her outfit, an appropriate blue heliotrope, so called because it turns to face the sun, and is thus a kind of clock. Yours and Maeterlinck's are red madder; conveniently, the best madder has always been grown in Holland and will thus lend credibility to his incognito. These are the colours of the two figures seen entering the room in van Eyck's mirror. Let us hope that you three enter it with equal ease. As for your return, here are three vials of Shamrock Tea; take them just before you wish to enter the painting at the other end.

93

HELIOTROPE

Fr Brown opened a door. The dressing rooms are in here, he said.

Maeterlinck and I were shown one room, Berenice another. Quickly, we divested ourselves of our uniforms and put on the unfamiliar apparel. When we emerged, Fr Brown beckoned to us to sit down, and continued his briefing.

Although your journey to fifteenth-century Bruges and back will seem instantaneous to us, he said, we do not know how much subjective time you will need in order to complete your mission. You will therefore need some money to sustain you; this, too, has been provided by our counterfeiters. You each have the equivalent of some thirty pounds sterling in present-day currency. Be sure not to spend it all at once. Here also is a plan of the city. Van Eyck's house is the one with the stone-gabled front with the carved heliotrope over the door, in the Sint Gillis Nieue Straet, now the Gouden Handt Straet, opposite the Schottinne Poorte. We have marked the spot with an X. But now, let us be quick! We have no time to lose.

Fr Brown moved swiftly into action, filling our tea-cups from the urn in the centre of the table, and handing us the clay pipes. The members of the Ancient Order likewise filled their cups.

Maeterlinck, Berenice and I began to drink and smoke. As the heady aroma of Shamrock Tea wafted into my nostrils, Fr Brown began to intone a Latin prayer; the others responded, the words swarming from their mouths, murmuring, growing in depth and resonance, until I found it difficult to tell the buzz in the room from that in my brain. I thought of tea-leaves boiling in a pot, the grains of noise in collapsing surf, a radio tuned to a dead frequency.

When I looked into my cup I found it empty, and I remembered being the age when a cup seemed the size of a soup bowl. I could see the flaws and bobbles in its huge glazed interior. The bottom was flecked with an archipelago of green strands which I thought might take years to explore. Then it occurred to me to look up. Tendrils of smoke rose from my pipe, some of them imprisoned in the air like wisps in ice, others like the swirl in a glass marble.

I caught Berenice's eye, then Maeterlinck's, and I believed we saw each other through each other's eyes, interlocked in one another's gaze.

Fr Brown's voice came to me from an immense distance. You are ready?

We nodded silently, and rose as one. Berenice took my left hand, and Maeterlinck's right. Together we approached the Arnolfini Double Portrait. The room became suddenly still and silent, but charged with electricity, as before the onset of a thunderstorm. The painting trembled, then began to grow, until it occupied the whole field of our vision. As we looked into the mirror on the back wall of the interior, the two figures in it blurred and vanished. We saw our three selves shimmer into focus in their stead.

I was shivering uncontrollably. Berenice's hand was icy cold on mine. Then I felt the power in my body connect up with hers, and through her I felt Maeterlinck, all our waves and particles swimming into one another. The three of us blinked; when we opened our eyes, we were suspended in deep black space, and our bodies had become interstellar dust.

All was utterly silent, but innumerable stars swarmed around us like voices. How long we drifted there I cannot tell. Perhaps it was an instant, perhaps eternity. What is time, when you are space itself? Whatever the case, before we could think about it, we were blown across the universe and out the other side.

We emerged in a high bare room.

94

IMPERIAL BLUE

Facing us, above an ornate marble fireplace, were two identical renderings of the Arnolfini Double Portrait. A one-legged, snub-nosed man of about forty, dressed in Regency clothing, was sleeping in an armchair by the empty grate. Before him, on an occasional table, was a half-empty bottle of brandy and a glass. The room was lit by a single tall window. Beyond it we could see the unmistakable silhouette of the Mourne Mountains.

The man wakened with a start. When he saw us, his face paled and a curious expression came into his eyes.

You are the three? he asked. Am I to be released?

Well, there are certainly three of us, replied Berenice. But to tell you the truth, we don't know what we are doing here, nor where exactly we are, nor even what the year is. Perhaps you could enlighten us.

With a trembling hand, the man poured himself a measure of brandy and tossed it back.

Regard the two portraits, he said. Do you note anything remarkable about them?

Well, they are, of course, identical, replied Berenice.

The man took a little mirror from his fob pocket and looked at himself, and then at the portraits. He shook his head sadly.

You think so? Perhaps you should hear my story. Would you like to?

We nodded our assent. The man poured himself another brandy, and began:

My name is Colonel James Hay, late of the 16th Light Dragoons in Wellington's army. It is the Feast of the Epiphany, in the Year of Our Lord 1817, and you find me in Castlemourne, County Down, the residence of Lady Mourne, to whom I am most grateful for her fine accommodations. My story begins on 21 June 1813, on which day, at Vittoria, in the province of Navarra, our forces completely routed the army of Joseph Bonaparte, erstwhile King of Naples and Spain. On the 23rd, some soldiers of my regiment intercepted a coach, whose blue livery proclaimed it to be the imperial vehicle of Joseph himself. By the time I arrived, accompanied by some of my officers, the men were too preoccupied by the cases of liquor to pay much attention to the other riches on board. Indeed, their chief prize was a parrot in a cage, which they had christened 'Vittoria'. The parrot, I must say, seemed remarkably quick, for already it was venturing to speak its new name, much to the delight of the troops.

We laid claim to three large chests of valuables, and that night, quartered in a bombed abbey, we played cards for the choice of the spoils. I remember a pair of silver-chased duelling pistols, four or five magnificent swords, a dinner service of gold plate, caskets full of jewellery and precious stones, a small library of books (most of which we burned), and a number of holy ikons, whose subjects were meaningless to me; but their lavishly orna-mented frames were worth a small fortune. There were also several other pictures of various dimensions, wrapped in red silk.

I had never been much of a one for papish observances; but a droll Irish fellow, a Lieutenant Patrick O'Flaherty, informed the company that it was St John's Eve, a most auspicious date. He proceeded to relate to us how the head of St John, at the behest of the dancing girl, Salome, was presented to her on a platter; as O'Flaherty talked, he acted the part of Herod, then that of Salome, cutting many a fine caper, the *pièce de résistance* being when he contrived, with the aid of a large gold serving-dish, to act the head of John.

It was a custom of his nation, he said, to mark the night of 23 June by smoking some stuff they called Shamrock Tea; would we do him the honour of sharing some with him, purely for medicinal purposes?

95

RED SILK

We were all in fine fettle, having gone through a bottle or two of Bonaparte's brandy, and we readily agreed to this proposition. Without further ado, the Irishman produced a little japanned tin snuff-box and a clay pipe, and lit up. He inhaled deeply a few times and passed the pipe to his neighbour, who did likewise.

Now, we had unwrapped the pictures and ranged them up against the wall, the better to appreciate them; though, if truth be told, we were the sort of fellows who judged a painting with a horse in it to be superior to one without a horse. Among the pictures was one of the pair you see in this room. I had paid little heed to it until then, but when it came my turn to smoke O'Flaherty's weed, it began fully to engage my attention. The more I looked at it, the more I felt I could walk into its interior, and I was fascinated by what might lie beyond the window.

We began to play. I shall not trouble you with the finer points of écarté, but I played the game of my life; I can still see every card I held that night. And I swear I could see the other fellows' cards reflected in their eyes. The first choice of the booty fell to me: I chose the painting over precious stones or weapons. I propped the painting at the foot of my makeshift bed, lay down and shut my eyes.

For a while I drifted on the border of sleep. I could still hear the sound of shot and shell, and the screams of the wounded, and see the gunsmoke rolling across the red earth of Spain. Into my mind sprang the image of one man, whose head rested on a heap of apples, his knees drawn up to his chin, his eyes wide open, seeming to inspect the head of a Frenchman, which, blown clean off, lay like a cannonball on his lap.

I opened my eyes in order to dispel this unpleasant sight. I found myself looking straight into the picture. The colours in it seemed to glow like gems, and I thought with satisfaction how I had gained the richest prize in King Joseph's treasury. Here was contentment and wealth. I saw myself in the enormous scarlet bed, or in the orchard beyond the window, plucking ripe cherries from the trees. Later I would stroll through the market-places of the peaceful city, before returning to this chamber, where everything was mine.

Then my very soul entered the painting, and I became the man in the painting, looking down at myself. And, as I looked, the features of the man lying on a pallet in a bombed Spanish abbey began to change. The face became longer, paler, the nostrils flared, like those of a horse, the eyes veiled. I was looking at the head of the man in the painting.

A bugle sounded, and I woke. I looked at the picture: it seemed to me that the expression of the man had subtly changed.

When I shaved that morning, my own face appeared unusually pale and gaunt. My hand shook and I cut myself on the upper lip. When I looked at the painting, sure enough, it, too, bore a trickle of blood in the corresponding spot.

O'Flaherty, I cried, come and see this!

O'Flaherty came over and stared at the picture.

What are you talking about, man? he said.

Look! The blood!

O'Flaherty looked at me quizzically.

The blood, your granny! he exclaimed, and he wetted his finger and picked a thread of red silk off the picture.

No more Shamrock Tea for you, he said, and went off laughing to himself.

96

BORDEAUX RED

Before long the picture began to show itself in its true colours. On 1 July – it was, O'Flaherty informed me, the feast of Oliver Plunket, whose embalmed head is enshrined in a Romanist chapel at Drogheda – we were visited by Wellington, who wished to discuss our further pursuit of the retreating French. We were quartered in a wine-cellar in Pamplona and the picture was propped up against my makeshift desk.

Remarkable likeness, Hay, said the Duke. Family heirloom, or what?

I stammered that I had only recently acquired it.

Wellington raised an eyebrow, and went on to outline his strategy.

On 3 July, I again cut myself shaving; and again a wound appeared on the chin of the man in the picture. I studied it carefully before summoning O'Flaherty, who attempted to pick off what he imagined to be another silk thread. No sooner had he touched the spot than he drew back as if stung, clutching his forefinger. It was bleeding profusely. When he saw this he went pale.

It is the feast day of St Thomas, he whispered, who doubted the wound in Christ's side.

The next day I had a stout canvas bag made up, and in this I concealed the picture. Nevertheless, it continued to haunt my dreams; every time I looked at it, the man seemed to resemble me more and more. After one particularly unpleasant night in which the dog in the picture emerged from the bag and attempted to bite my legs, I resolved to get rid of my hard-won prize. We were leaving Pamplona that morning; I left it behind in a niche of the wine-cellar.

When we reached our destination of San Estavan, we took up quarters in the sacristy of a church dedicated to St John the Baptist. There, in the corner, was the canvas bag. I knew without opening it that the picture would be inside. I opened it anyway, and it seemed that the face of the man – who was myself, yet not myself – wore a sardonic grin. I asked O'Flaherty for advice. He could only suggest that since praying to St Antony of Padua was effective in restoring lost articles, cursing him might do the trick in my case. This I tried to no avail; perhaps I lacked the requisite faith.

I tried other methods. I weighted the bag with stones and sank it in the Bidassoa river. We marched on to Lesaca, where we took up quarters in the crypt of a ruined monastery. I found the picture lying on the tombstone of a Spanish count. Then I toyed with the idea of tying it to the mouth of a cannon and blowing it to smithereens; but I feared that by doing so I might destroy myself. So I reconciled myself to its inevitable presence.

Time passed. I grew to think of the picture as a partner in a reluctant but workable marriage. Often I would deliberately abandon it, secure in the knowledge that it would confront me at my next billet. Indeed, I looked upon it as a guarantee of my safe conduct, and of my future existence: for wherever the picture would be, I was bound to follow.

We crossed the Pyrenees at the pretty town of St Jean de Luz, and quartered at the chateau of Arcangues. On 9 November, the feast of Theodore the Recruit, patron of the military, we engaged the French. The result was inconclusive; but by now, the war was effectively over. In the New Year, we marched on to Toulouse, Plaisance and Bordeaux, where we embarked for English soil at last, on the feast of Oliver Plunket, 1 July 1814.

97

WHITE LINEN

Quartered in Dover barracks, our men soon forgot the fatigues of the Peninsular campaigns. Peace became irksome to them and they grew impatient for fresh exploits; nor were they long disappointed. In March 1815 news reached London that Napoleon had broken free from his retirement in Elba and had marched audaciously into Paris, where he had regrouped his forces. On 4 May, the feast of St Florian of Austria, we received orders to embark for Ostend, where we arrived safe. From thence we proceeded into Bruges, arriving on 7 May, the feast of St Domitian of Maastricht, who is invoked against dragons.

Bruges is a city of shadows. Bells ring mournfully at all hours of the day, their echoes trembling in the dead canals. It is a city of reflections, and its past is mirrored in the tall windows of the burghers' houses. O'Flaherty and I were given fine rooms in the Rue de la Main d'Or. I had not looked on the picture for some time. I drew it out of its cover and, as I regarded it with a mixture of trepidation and familiarity, the concièrge, who was helping us with our things, let out a little gasp of astonishment. Thus I learned that the picture had come home; for he told me that the Johannes de Eyck who had signed it had been resident in that very street in 1434.

That night, for the first time, the lady in the picture entered my dreams. I woke exhausted. We were to depart for Ghent that morning; hastily, I packed and we boarded the canal boat. It was misty. As the flat countryside glided by, it seemed we were poised on a motionless border, beyond which lay an undiscovered realm. When we arrived, my first action was to take out the canvas bag. As I did so, it went limp in my hands. De Eyck's picture was not there.

I felt as if my soul had been drained from me. But what could I do? I could not return; I was a soldier and rumours of Napoleon's imminent presence were rife. The next day, we received orders to march for Brussels, and there I remained for some weeks, a shadow of my former self, sleepwalking through my daily business. Then, on 18 June, the feast of the twin martyrs Mark and Marcellian, orders came to meet Napoleon at the village of Waterloo. I felt no fear, for my body was not my own.

O'Flaherty, who was by my side, was decapitated by chain-shot. As for myself, a cannonball took away my right leg. Later I was told that the wound was so bad that I could not be moved for eight days. That I had survived at all was a miracle, they said. Perhaps, for as I lay there, the lady from the picture came to me and bandaged my stump with her linen headdress. When I was taken to Brussels to recuperate, they put me in a room in which hung a painting of a man and a woman with their hands joined. The de Eyck had returned to me; or I was returned to it.

As for the rest, I will be brief. Now the couple in the painting haunted me more than ever, for I owed them my life. In exchange, they demanded to meet their twins, who they said resided in Ireland. The curious thing was, though I knew they spoke in either French or Flemish, languages which are largely unintelligible to me, I heard them in my inward ear as English. I set out for Ireland on 20 August 1815, the feast of Bernard of Clairvaux, the patron saint of bees.

I wandered this country for some months, until I arrived in the vicinity of Castlemourne. Now the couple became tremendously excited, and I guessed I was close to my destination. I presented myself to Lady Mourne, who appeared not unpleased with my company, and, on 7 December, the feast of St Ambrose, the patron of beekeepers, I was led to this ante-room, wherein I found the picture's twin.

98

MYRRH

But still the picture would not release me, continued Colonel Hay. The couple now came up with another condition, which I heard in a rhyme, as follows:

> *We have no power to set you free*
> *Unless you meet the children three –*
> *Two in red and one in blue*
> *Are present, past, and future too.*

And that, concluded Colonel Hay, is my story. What do you make of it?

Maeterlinck put up his hand.

One thing, sir, he said, is clear. We are all implicated in the case of Shamrock Tea, and of the Double Portrait, which might be described as a translating device. I use 'translating' according to its Latin etymology, which means to carry over or to transfer from one place or condition to another. Hence the relics of saints, when brought from their resting place to be installed in a dedicated altar, or even when stolen from one church by the priests of another, are said to be translated. But before we broach this topic further, which is the van Eyck you procured at Vittoria, and which is the other?

Colonel Hay looked at the two pictures.

By Jove! he exclaimed. I cannot tell them apart!

He pulled out his pocket mirror and looked at himself.

I am myself again! he cried.

That is all very well, said Maeterlinck drily. However, this state of affairs presents us with a problem, for we arrived in this room by way of one device, whereas we now have two. As a military man you will appreciate that we cannot discuss our mission with you in any great detail, for it is of a highly secret nature. All we can tell you is that we were supposed to be in Bruges in 1434, and not in County Down in 1817.

It would seem you have got lost in translation, murmured Colonel Hay. But seriously, you are forgetting one thing. After I acquired the painting, and my relationship with it began to deepen, I learned more and more to trust in the calendar of saints, as indicated to me by poor O'Flaherty – God rest his soul! – for it is a kind of universal time-scale, by which the future is always indicated by the past. Indeed, Lady Mourne's confessor, the Revd Ignatius Doyle, S.J., has been instructing me in the finer points of Augustinian philosophy, and has indicated that I shall soon be ready to be received into the One Holy Catholic Apostolic Roman Church. You will remember that I told you that it is the feast of the Epiphany, that is, of the three travelling Magi, Caspar, Balthazar and Melchior. It is truly a red-letter day. I refer you to the second chapter of Matthew, where they present the Christ child with gifts of gold, frankincense and myrrh. And then, *Being warned of God in a dream that they should not return to Herod, they departed into their own country another way.*

So, for you three there will always be a way, which will lead you to the country that you seek. *In my Father's house are many mansions*, saith the Lord. Given that infinity of worlds, you need not deliberate about a choice of rooms. Only make the leap of faith and you will arrive at where you were meant to be.

Your logic, said Maeterlinck, is most persuasive. And besides, what have we got to lose?

He looked at Berenice and me.

We nodded wordlessly. We took the Shamrock Tea, and faced the two Double Portraits.

After a while, I felt my body shimmer and dissolve. Which of the pictures I entered, I cannot tell. I never saw Berenice or Maeterlinck again.

99

CHAMELEON

According to a series of accounts in the *Gazette van Gent* of November 1952, the sacristan of the Cathedral of St Bavon, while making his rounds at the close of All Souls' Day, discovered a boy of about thirteen lying unconscious immediately beneath the altarpiece known as *The Adoration of the Immaculate Lamb*, which had only recently been restored to its full glory. The *Gazette* took this opportunity of reminding its readers of the numerous vicissitudes this most imposing work of the early Flemish school had suffered in its history, having been banished by the Protestant iconoclasts in the sixteenth century, stolen by French revolutionaries at the turn of the eighteenth century, restored to Ghent after the Battle of Waterloo, the shutters sold off by a Vicar-General of the diocese to the King of Prussia shortly afterwards, but reunited to the central panels by the Treaty of Versailles, after which the work enjoyed comparative peace, until stolen again by the Hitler regime and confined to the Altaussee salt mine in Austria, from whence it was liberated by American troops.

The boy, when eventually revived, appeared to be bereft of the faculty of speech. His curious medieval garb prompted some speculation that he might be a member of a travelling circus, but enquiries in this field elicited no response. Comparisons were then drawn with the enigmatic case of Kaspar Hauser, who was found by the Haller gate of the city of Nuremberg on Whit Monday, 26 May 1828, and whose language was little else but unintelligible sounds, mixed with tears and moans, so that the usual questions, such as, What is your name? Where did you come from? Produce your passport! were put to the youth in vain. A close scrutiny of his attire increased the mystery, for it consisted of a peasant's jacket over a coarse shirt, a groom's pantaloons, and a white handkerchief marked K. H. The contents of his pockets created the greatest surprise. They consisted of some coloured rags, a key, a paper twist of gold sand, a small horn rosary, and a number of pictures of saints. Here the comparisons with the boy found in Ghent broke down, for there were no pockets to his garments. However, a leather purse attached to his belt contained thirty silver coins, which were found to be counterfeits of the currency stabilized by Philip the Good in 1434.

A later item in the *Gazette* of 26 April 1953 noted that the boy, like Kaspar Hauser, had almost fully recovered his faculties, and was now able to speak fluently and intelligibly, though, like Hauser, his memory of his origin was as yet obscure. The *Gazette* promised to report further on the boy's progress, but no such report was ever filed.

So it was that I found myself in the world I now inhabit. Confused as I was for some months, I only gradually learned that it was not the same world as that I had left, although it was almost identical in most respects. The same constellations shone in its skies. Its light conformed to the same colour spectrum. The same countries were delineated on its maps, and their history was just as troubled; the same wars had been fought. Pope Pius XII was the head of the Roman Catholic Church, which maintained the same calendar of saints, though it was not as religiously observed as it had been in my former world. The same flora and fauna abounded, and herbs had the same properties.

Wanting to blend in with my hosts, I learned to speak Flemish and French; I reserved English for my private thoughts. The sensational nature of my case brought me briefly to the attention of an adoring public, and I was adopted by a wealthy art-dealer of Ghent, named Henri Maeterlinck. In deference to him, and in honour of the Maeterlinck whose loss I still mourn, I took that name as mine. I was sent to the Collège de Sainte-Barbe in Ghent and spent my summers in Oostacker, where I amused myself by studying my guardian's bees. I learned to become another person.

100

BIBLE BLACK

I began to research my new world. I discovered that only one Arnolfini Double Portrait was known to exist, in the National Gallery in London, which acquired it from a Colonel James Hay in the year 1842. Hay died in 1854, in which year Oscar Wilde and Edward Carson were born. I have been to see the Double Portrait twice; each time, I was disappointed, for it is covered by glass, and I was distracted by the reflections of its onlookers, and by my own. I bought several reproductions of it; in each, the colours were subtly wrong. Eventually I burned them.

There were several Carsons in Belfast, but no Celestine, or Berenice, or me. There was no Loyola House; or rather, there once had been a version of it. I found the following account in George Basset's Directory of County Down of 1886:

Thomas Percy, author of the *Key to the New Testament*, etc., was Bishop of Dromore for nearly thirty years, from 1782. Loyola House, in the vicinity of the town, was for many years the palace of Bishop Percy, whose taste in planning is manifest to this day in the beautifully wooded hills forming a demesne of 211 statute acres. The property was purchased from the Church Temporalities Commissioners by Messrs. Edward and James Quinn, whose remains are entombed in the cathedral churchyard. The Jesuit Fathers purchased of the executors of the brothers in 1883, and the former palace was opened in the following year as a novitiate house for the Society of Jesus in Ireland.

More recently, the authoritative C. E. B. Brett, in his *Survey of the Towns and Villages of Mid Down*, has this to say:

When, in 1842, the diocese of Dromore was merged with those of Down and Connor, the Palace was sold; after 1883 an attempt was made to establish a Jesuit school there under the name 'Loyola House', but it did not succeed; since then the house has remained 'untenanted and desolate'. Since the last war the trees have all been cut down, and the formerly handsome foursquare Georgian house, one of the centres of literary and artistic enlightenment in Ireland, has now come to the last and saddest stage of dissolution and decay.

I made no attempt to visit Ireland. Instead, I devoted my energies to becoming a model citizen of my new nation. Upon leaving the Collège de Sainte-Barbe, I attended the University of Louvain, where, after graduating with honours in English Literature, I took a Master's degree in Librarianship, after which I undertook an apprenticeship in the Ghent Public Library. I was pleased to find that its collection held a first edition of Voltaire's *Zadig*; I was struck again by how this world and the other lay so close together, tissue-thin, like two adjacent pages in a Bible, yet stuck irretrievably together, never to be opened.

I recalled Colonel Hay's saying, *In my Father's house are many mansions*; and in my dreams I would wander again the precincts of Loyola House. I would turn a corner, and there, at the end of the corridor, I would see Berenice. I would run towards her with my arms open; but before I reached her, she would turn into an aged nun, and I would wake, my eyes blinded by tears, a universe away from her.

I was overjoyed when, on the feast day of Catherine of Alexandria, 1963, I was informed that my application for the post of Director of the Hospice Library in Gheel had been successful.

101

BLANK

I have reached a kind of equilibrium in myself. This world is not perfect, but neither was the one from which I am an exile. My position in Gheel allows me to explore the mystery of personality; for in Gheel it is difficult to know who is mad and who is sane. My closest friends call themselves by names they have learned from books; and, versed as I am in literature, I can perfectly accommodate their pictures of themselves. Yesterday, Sherlock Holmes and I discussed again the ramifications of the case of the Six Napoleons, and I offered Napoleon himself an alternative outcome to the Battle of Quatre Bras on 16 June 1815, which would have significantly altered that of Waterloo, two days later. Dioscorides has been of inestimable worth in my researches into Shamrock Tea; his discovery that cinquefoil combined with aconite affects our personal perception of time is a major breakthrough. St Augustine has shown some interest in these findings, since they offer some support to his notion that time is memory.

Wittgenstein calls on me daily. Sometimes he sits in silence for many hours, before uttering a gnomic sentence, whose meaning eludes me for some days. But when I restate it, he brushes it aside impatiently, saying that he was a fool to think of it in the first place. At other times, he excitedly embarks on a long and detailed philosophical paradigm. For example, today, he ventured the following:

Imagine that there is a town in which the policemen are required to obtain information from each inhabitant, for example, his name, his age, where he came from, his occupation, his pastimes, his associates, and the like. A record is kept of this information, and some use is made of it; for in this imaginary town, it is important to know what the inhabitants might do or plan in any given circumstance. Occasionally, when a policeman questions an inhabitant, he discovers that the latter does not do any work, that he has no hobbies, that he has no known associates; in fact, let us go further and imagine that this inhabitant does not even know, or refuses to divulge, his name and age. The policeman enters these facts on record, for they, too, are useful pieces of information about the man! What do you think of that, my dear Maeterlinck? said Wittgenstein.

Perhaps, I said, were the policeman observant enough, he might also have added certain deductions he had made from the man's appearance. I understand from Holmes, for example, that cuffs, trouser-knees and boots afford certain clues to a man's occupation, or his previous occupation; that sleeves and thumbnails are most suggestive; and that nothing has more individuality than pipes, save, perhaps, watches and bootlaces.

Wittgenstein looked at me in some exasperation.

Clockwork! he cried. Mere pragmatic clockwork! And with this you suppose to penetrate the mystery of being? You know, Maeterlinck, perhaps you should write a book. A costume drama, in which the characters are described wholly in terms of their appearances, and which allows them no inner thoughts.

Indeed, I said, today I began to write a story. Yesterday I discovered, in the archive of this library, some childhood letters from my cousin, which I had believed to be lost forever. I have no idea how they got here, but I was reminded that, in the eyes of God, nothing is ever lost, for everything that ever was still is, for Him. I was deeply moved by the reappearance of this correspondence, and, for a moment, I glimpsed that lost world of my childhood in its entirety.

It struck me that I might use the resources of this library to construct a believable historical reality – a world which would differ only marginally from this one – using circumstantial detail of the kind you mention. Would you like me to read you the first few sentences?

Wittgenstein shrugged philosophically, and I began:

Perhaps I will return one day to the world I first entered. For now, I wish to record something of it, if only to remind myself of what I am.

The first things I remember are the colours of my bedroom wallpaper . . .

SELECTED SOURCES

For the lives of saints, my chief sources have been:

David Farmer, *The Oxford Dictionary of Saints*, O.U.P., 1997

Sean Kelly & Rosemary Rogers, *Saints Preserve Us!*, Robson Books, 1995

The Rev. Bernard Kelly ed., *Butler's Lives of the Fathers, Martyrs, and other Principal Saints*, Virtue and Company, 1961

Michael Walsh ed., *Butler's Lives of Patron Saints*, Burns and Oates, 1987

Donald Attwater, *The Penguin Dictionary of Saints*, Penguin Books, 1965

Rev. S. Baring-Gould, *The Lives of the Saints*, John Grant, 1914

Jacobus de Voragine, *The Golden Legend*, Princeton University Press, 1993

For St Dympna, and Gheel:

John Webster, 'Notes on Belgian Lunatic Asylums, including the Insane Colony of Gheel', in *The Journal of Psychological Medicine and Mental Pathology*, Jan. 1857

SELECTED SOURCES

Entry on St Dympna in John O'Hanlon, *The Lives of the Irish Saints*,
James Duffy & Sons, Dublin, 1875
Baedeker's Belgium and Holland, 1910

For van Eyck:
Linda Seidel, *Jan van Eyck's Arnolfini Portrait: Stories of an Icon*,
University of Chicago Press, 1993
Otto Pächt, *Van Eyck and the Founders of Early Netherlandish Painting*,
Harvey Miller Publishers, London, 1994
The Complete Paintings of the Van Eycks, with an introduction by Robert
Hughes, and notes and catalogue by Giorgio T. Faggin, Penguin
Books, 1968
Craig Harbinson, *Jan van Eyck: The Play of Realism*, Reaktion Books,
1991
Jean C. Wilson, *Painting in Bruges at the Close of the Middle Ages*,
Pennsylvania State University Press, 1998
Maurice W. Brockwell, *The Van Eyck Problem*, Chatto & Windus,
1954
William Henry James Weale, *The Van Eycks and their Art*, John Lane,
The Bodley Head, 1928
Elisabeth Dhanens, *Van Eyck: The Ghent Altarpiece*, Allen Lane, 1973
Ludwig von Baldass, *Jan van Eyck*, Phaidon Press, 1952
Edwin Hall, *The Arnolfini Betrothal: Medieval Marriage and the Enigma
of van Eyck's Double Portrait*, University of California Press, 1997
Erwin Panofsky, *Early Netherlandish Painting: Its Origins and Character*,
Harper & Row, New York, 1971
Lorne Campbell, *The Fifteenth-century Netherlandish Schools*, National
Gallery, London, 1998

For Ludwig Wittgenstein (besides his own works):
Ray Monk, *Ludwig Wittgenstein*, Jonathan Cape, 1990
M. O'C. Drury, *The Danger of Words*, Thoemmes Press, 1996

John Heaton & Judy Groves, *Wittgenstein for Beginners*, Icon Books, 1994

Marjorie Perloff, *Wittgenstein's Ladder*, University of Chicago Press, 1996

W.W. Bartley, *Ludwig Wittgenstein*, Open Court, 1985

Brian McGuinness, *Wittgenstein: A Life. Young Ludwig 1889–1921*, Duckworth, 1988

Norman Malcolm, *Ludwig Wittgenstein: A Memoir* (with a Biographical Sketch by G.H. von Wright), O.U.P., 1984

For Arthur Conan Doyle (besides his own works):

Owen Dudley Edwards, *The Quest for Sherlock Holmes*, Penguin Books, 1984

Michael Harrison, *The World of Sherlock Holmes*, New English Library, 1975

Jack Tracy, *The Ultimate Sherlock Holmes Encyclopaedia*, Gramercy Books, 1977

For Gerard Manley Hopkins:

Gerard Manley Hopkins, *Journals and Papers*, Humphrey House ed., completed by Graham Storey, Oxford University Press, 1959

Norman White, *Hopkins: A Literary Biography*, Clarendon Press, 1992

Paddy Kitchen, *Gerard Manley Hopkins: A Life*, Carcanet, 1989

For Oscar Wilde (besides his own works):

Richard Ellman, *Oscar Wilde*, Hamilton, 1987

E.K. Mikhail ed., *Oscar Wilde, Interviews and Recollections*, Macmillan, 1989

The character of 'Maeterlinck' was suggested by some aspects of the life of the Belgian writer Maurice Maeterlinck (1862–1949). Among the works consulted were:

SELECTED SOURCES

Maurice Maeterlinck, *The Life of the Bee* (Des Abeilles), translated by
Alfred Sutro, George Allen & Unwin, 1901

W.D. Halls, *Maurice Maeterlinck*, Clarendon Press, 1960

Gaston Compère, *Maurice Maeterlinck*, La Manufacture, Paris, 1990

The quotations attributed to St Augustine are based on R.S. Pine-Coffin's translation of the *Confessions* (Penguin Books, 1961).

I would also like to acknowledge some specific sources to the text:

p. 2 **On 20 July 1434 . . .** Based on an account in J.A.
McCulloch, *Medieval Faith and Fable*, Harrap & Co., 1932

p. 14 **Cennino** See *The Craftsman's Handbook*, translated by Daniel
V. Thompson, Jr., Dover Books, 1960

p. 17 **Wittgenstein** This passage is a conflation of two almost
identical passages in Ludwig Wittgenstein, *Remarks on Colour*, ed.
G.E.M. Anscombe, Blackwell, 1977

pp. 82–85 Wittgenstein's dreams are adapted from accounts in
W.W. Bartley.

pp. 104–105 **Company of Jesus** See Lord Macauley, *Ranke's
History of the Popes*, Edinburgh Review, October 1840

pp. 113–116 The story of Uncle Franck is adapted from an
account in Julian Barnes, *Flaubert's Parrot* (pp. 57–58 in the
Picador edition, 1985)

p. 127 **von Frisch** See Karl von Frisch, *The Dancing Bees: An
Account of the Life and Senses of the Honey Bee*, Methuen, 1966

p. 135 **Th' industrious bee . . .** quoted in Eva Crane, *The
Archaeology of Beekeeping*, Duckworth, 1983

pp. 137–143 My version of *Zadig* is indebted to chapter 4 of *Zadig,
and Other Romances*, translated by H.I. Woolf, Routledge, n.d.
My inclusion of the story was prompted by a reading of several
essays in *The Sign of Three: Dupin, Holmes, Peirce*, edited by Umberto
Eco and Thomas A. Sebeok, Indiana University Press, 1983

p. 154 **unicorn . . .**   See 'From Marco Polo to Leibniz: Stories of Intellectual Misunderstandings', in Umberto Eco, *Serendipities*, Weidenfield & Nicolson, 1999

p. 158 **passages of great beauty . . .**   This paragraph, and p. 160, para. 2, are adapted from Antoine de St. Éxupery, *Night Flight* (Vol de Nuit), translated by Curtis Cate (with acknowledgements to Stuart Gilbert's translation), Heinemann Educational Books, 1971

p. 161 **Schubert**   My translation of the Schubert song is based on that in John Reed, *The Schubert Song Companion*, (with prose translations by Norma Deane & Celia Larner) Manchester University Press, 1985

p. 163 **Ansel Bourne**   See William James, *The Principles of Psychology*, Macmillan, 1891; also Henri F. Ellenberger, *The Discovery of the Unconscious*, pp. 134–135, Allen Lane, The Penguin Press, 1970

p. 172 **Mary Reynolds**   Ibid., pp. 128–129

p. 174 **St. Paul's Church . . .**   Ibid., p. 123

p. 202 **They are taken into cots . . .**   See Rainer Maria Rilke, 'Reflections on Dolls', in *Rodin and Other Prose Pieces*, Quartet Books, 1986

p. 233 **Once upon a time . . .**   See *Oscar Wilde, Interviews and Recollections*, Macmillan, 1989

p. 296 **Kaspar Hauser**   See *Chambers's Miscellany of Useful and Entertaining Tracts*, Vol. V, Edinburgh, 1845

p. 299 **C.E.B. Brett**   This quotation is by kind permission of the author

p. 302 **Imagine that there is a town . . .**   adapted from a quotation in Norman Malcolm